THREE-SMILE MILE

by

Chad Lutzke

CHAD LUTZKE

Print edition

Copyright © 2023 Chad Lutzke, Static Age Books

ALL RIGHTS RESERVED

Cover Design by Chad Lutzke

This is a work of fiction. Names, characters, business, places, events and incidents are either the products of the author's imagination or used in a fictitious manner. Any resemblance to actual persons, living or dead, or actual events is purely coincidental.

To subscribe to my newsletter, visit www.chadlutzke.com

To become a supportive patron and receive exclusive content, visit

www.patreon.com/ChadLutzke

CHAPTER 1: CAKE
Glover, Texas

Cake presses the spatula down on the burger patty, and the grill sizzle-hisses like a thousand angry bees. Grease splashes on his wrist. Pinpricks he's gotten used to.

He throws the patty on a bun prepared with mayo, lettuce, pickle, and a tomato that should have been thrown out yesterday, then puts it on a plate with an order of steak fries and rings the bell, letting Lucille know the order's up.

"Thanks, hon'," Lucille says. Hon is her favorite word, Cake thinks. Not so much during the bar rush, when the assholes pour in, propped up on legs made from draft beer and diluted shots.

His eyes are on the woman in booth C. Early-to-mid thirties. She's with an older guy who looks like a real dick. Maybe mid-forties. He's not too ugly. But Cake doesn't like the way he gazes out the window while the woman talks, like he couldn't give a shit.

When Cake finally catches the woman's eye, he smiles. There's a shitload of words in the smile. *I'm sorry you're with him. You deserve better. I get off at 10:00.*

She smiles back. He's not sure what her smile says. Maybe, *Thanks. I'm trapped. By the way, where's my eggs?*

He grabs four eggs, cracks them over the griddle. A thousand angry bees. He looks back. The woman is lighting a cigarette, being careful where she blows the smoke, waving her hand to summon the cloud away from the man. She's wearing a wedding ring. So is he.

Cake thinks they're probably married, that the man once pulled her out of a bad relationship, looking like the hero. Now he's forgotten the hunt. He doesn't pursue her anymore. No longer wears cologne. Burps and farts, pisses on the seat, only holds her hand when they're in bed. And it's not really her hand but her wrist. And not out of love but lust, as he holds her down.

It's a lot to assume, but as a grill cook

for a diner on Route 66, the game helps pass the time.

"There's no cheese, Cake," Lucille says. She's got two pencils in her hair, one above each ear, because she never remembers which side it's on.

Cake snaps out of his trance. "Huh?"

"Ain't no cheese on this burger. You forgot the cheese." Lucille recently fell in love with a man named Deke—a truckdriver passing through, swept her off her feet. Cake thinks about how much she deserves it.

He grabs the plate, opens the bun, tosses on a slice of processed cheese. Pure American.

"If they bitch because it's not melted, I'm sending them your way," Lucille says.

"Want me to nuke it?"

"Hell no. There's lettuce and tomato on here."

"Well, leave it a minute. It'll melt."

"I'm not sacrificing a tip so's you don't get the third degree. Instead, how about you pay attention to what the fuck yer doin'." She grabs the plate and whips around the counter with the finesse of an ice skater.

Lucille isn't trying to be mean, but when it gets busy like this, she's all out of "hons." Really, she looks out for Cake, covers for him when he shows up late. Lied for him the time he fed the kitten out back, told her boss it was Thomas Geren who did it, the regular who grabs her ass every time he's within two feet of it. Grabbed so hard one time her panties went up her asshole. Thomas about lost a tooth over that one.

The clock says it's just about time the boss shows up, so the machine needs to appear well oiled, running smoothly. And when it isn't, Cake is the target. Always.

When Cake put his application in two years ago, it was to be temporary. Three months temporary. Just enough for first-month's rent and deposit, then he'd look elsewhere. But routine, convenience, and the fear of change has a way of clamping down. Barbed wire around an old tree, choking the ever-living shit out of goals and dreams.

Eyes on the woman again as thick slabs of bacon spit fireworks on his wrist. The woman looks at him a second time.

Smiles. He thinks this smile might say friendlier words. *He may be my husband, but I don't love him anymore.* Or, *you sure do look good for a cook.*

Over the past two years, Cake has cast eyes on countless women sitting at the booths, but not once grabbing their attention—excluding, of course, Brenda, who came in drunk at 10:00 p.m., right at quitting time. She'd made a promise to herself to lay the first man who so much as glanced her way, after having caught her boyfriend in bed with a high school girl. Brenda wasn't pretty. She wasn't even kind. She was just there, and sometimes all it takes is a little seductive attention for a man to lose his ability to say no. And within the hour, Cake wished he had. Feeling cheap, dirty, and a little used ain't no way to start a day.

But this woman smiled back. This older woman. And a returning smile holds power, kicks the attraction up from wishful thinking to a potential happening. Sweat. Skin on skin. Or hell, some pleasant conversation and a goodnight kiss. Cake is fine with that. He's been lonely far too long.

But she's married, or so it seems, yet something isn't right. For starters, she isn't happy. Cake is good at reading body language, watching all number of characters across that counter while the grease licks his forearms, he gets to know people well. And the way this woman moves her mouth, fidgets with the fork she doesn't need yet—*eggs will be done soon, hon'.* And even the way she inhales the smoke from her cigarette—which he doesn't notice until she lights up a second—smoking like she hasn't had one all week, drawing in deep, blowing out like she wishes she could hold it just a little bit longer. Not only is she not happy. She's stuck.

CHAPTER 2: DIANE

Diane smiles at the cook for the third time, the corner of her lip curling in a way that says, *take me back behind this greasy diner and fuck me silly*. Her husband Conner recognizes the smile, because it's the same one she used on him six months ago. Exactly two months before they were married.

She liked the way he ignored her, pretended to be disinterested when they met at Susan Graffo's wedding. Conner was there as someone else's date, and they left the reception early. Together. They spent the next two months in every hotel between Amarillo and Nacogdoches, rarely leaving the room. Rarely getting dressed. She thought it was love. So, when he proposed, she said yes. Deep down. Deep, deep down, wasn't it every girl's dream to be with a man who lived a reckless life, never knowing what tomorrow might bring? Someone who knew when to bend her over the table and when to play it nice, offering a sweet caress, a kiss on the forehead.

Diane thought Conner knew that, but he only has one gear, and it's high. A month into their marriage and the passion was gone. For her it was. The dangerous excitement had become old hat, and now she's grown to despise him. He's a man-boy in her eyes. A quick dick, fast car, and a penchant for rebellion only goes so far. Now she wants a sweet man. One who tears up at his favorite song, that one part in the chorus that puts a tingle in his spine. A man who holds a legitimate job. One who loves his mother because she raised him right, taught him about chivalry and sacrifice.

But this thing with Conner. This shit marriage. There's no end in sight, and now she's grown scared of him. The first night she'd turned him down for sex, that was the last time. He hadn't hurt her (not yet), but she saw it in his eyes. *What? You think now that we're married you don't gotta give it up?*

And that time at The Gangplank, when the guy at the bar held his stare a little too long. Conner broke the man's nose and snapped his ankle. *She's mine, motherfucker!*

Til death do they part.

"Take me to Disney Land, Conner. I never got to go as a little girl." Diane twirls long blonde hair on her finger. She knows his weakness. Act defenseless, innocent. In need. Giving him the power, like he's the only one who can brighten her day, make her dreams come true, put a sparkle in her eye. "It'll be fun."

Conner looks out the window. "You're too old for that silly shit. You're a woman. Act like it."

"It's not just for kids, you know. They have rides, and shops, and restaurants. They have an area that's decorated like the Orient. We could eat Japanese food, and you could buy me a souvenir. It'd be romantic."

"Or we could skip the kiddie bullshit and head for the hotel, break the bed in."

She lights another cigarette. "That all you ever think about? Sex?"

His eyes drift to hers. His foot reaches

out and meets hers under the table. "My favorite pastime."

She huffs and rolls her eyes. "Well, I'm bored. I'm bored of—" She stops, knowing that speaking her mind is a mistake. The words hang from the cliff of her tongue: *I'm bored of you and your one-speed fucking, of the whole gangster thing with your gun and your crime and your bullshit suits, and that stupid car you baby like it's Mother Teresa on wheels.* "Sorry, I'm just hungry."

"Me too. How long's it take to make some hashbrowns and eggs, anyway?" He throws his hand in the air. "Hey, lady. What's the deal with our order?"

Diane shouldn't have mentioned the food. Now he's going to make a scene.

"Hey, kid! Hurry it up in there!"

"Conner, please don't."

"Why? Because you think he's cute?" Conner laughs, almost maniacally. "What? You think I didn't notice? Three times you gave him my smile. Three. Once is polite. Two and you're sending a message. Three and you're already picking out a hotel."

"Are you serious? I'm a married woman. You're my husband."

"Don't give me that shit." He lifts his arm again, waves his hand. "Hey, kid! You wanna fuck my wife?"

Customers swing their heads toward the couple. The cook ignores him.

"Hey, kid!"

"Sir," the waitress says. "People are trying to eat. You'll have your food in a minute."

Diane covers the side of her face, hiding behind her hand, and looks out the window at nothing at all. "Conner, please stop." The words squeeze through gritting teeth.

"I don't take that shit, baby. You know that."

"Yes, I do know that. But there's nothing to worry about. He's just a cook in a grease-hole dive."

"Then keep your fuckin' eyes to yourself." Conner slams his hand on the table, gets up, and heads for the restroom.

CHAPTER 3: CAKE

If the boss-man were here, this is the kind of thing that would be a strike against Cake. Doesn't matter that it's not his fault. Boss-man would never see how it really is: an entitled, possibly drunk, macho asshole with a complex, trying to start shit with a man he feels threatened by, both in age and looks. Middle-aged men get like that. They hate younger people because they want to be them. They want to relive the carefree days. They want the stamina back, the kind where they could fuck for an hour, run four miles, then fuck again. Scarf down a grocery bag full of junk food and a six pack, then go yet another round with a girl whose tits point north and a snatch that hasn't lost its grip to an eight-pound baby.

"Hey, kid!"

Cake thinks about spitting in the eggs, but he isn't sure who ordered them.

Lucille leans on the counter. "You

checkin' his wife out, Cake?"

"Just being friendly is all."

"Well, cut it out and keep your eye on the grill. What'd I tell you about paying attention."

Twenty-two years old, and he's in high school again. Except his bully is a forty-nine-year-old woman with pencils in her hair and a chest that could suffocate a rhino.

"You got their order done yet?"

Cake throws the last bit of hashbrowns onto one of the plates. "Yep." He sets it on the counter that divides the kitchen from the checkout.

"Good. Go take it to her. I just got rushed and don't have time."

"I can't go over there, Lucille."

"You can, and you will." She turns to leave, reaching for one of the pencils in her hair.

Cake looks at the booth. The man is gone, and the woman stares out the window, blowing a cloud of smoke from her lungs. *Dammit.* He looks around the diner, scans the parking lot through the giant windows. No sign of the guy.

Before the guy shows up again, Cake grabs the plates and walks through the swinging kitchen door, moving quickly toward booth C and the woman who'd sent so many seductive words his way in the form of three smiles.

His eyes are on the parking lot, another look around the diner. Bumps into a customer walking toward the door, excuses himself. "Sorry."

The plates hit the table hard enough to startle the woman. She jumps. She's on edge.

"Sorry," Cake says again, then turns to leave. He doesn't want to look at her. The smiles were taboo, and they'd gotten caught. Long-distance adultery. Mind fucks. The affair is over.

A hand grabs his wrist. "Wait." He can feel the cold of her wedding band against his skin. "What's your name?" This older woman has her eyes on the restroom, her leg moving up and down like a jackhammer, like it's trying to start a fire under the table.

He doesn't want to pull his wrist away. Whether he's reveling in this micro attention from a female at last, or because he hates the guy who's about to catch him, he's not sure. But he doesn't move. "Cake."

"Cake?" She's finally looking at him now.

"Yeah."

"Okay, Cake. I'm Diane. Do you like working here?"

"No. I hate it. I should be somewhere else."

She looks back to the restroom. "Yeah, me too. Listen, you seem like a good kid…"

"I'm twenty-two."

"That's a kid to me, sweetie."

"But I'm not."

"Okay, Mr. Twenty-Two-Year-Old Cake. Do you wanna leave this place?"

"Are you offering me a job?"

"No, I'm offering you a new life." Her leg stops jackhammering. Every word she says is made of concrete. She's only looking at him now, deep into his eyes. Whatever this woman—this older woman—is going to say next, she means it with everything in her. That's what her eyes are saying. Every bit of her. Her gaze is a living thing that dwells within him. It's fucking vampiric.

"Cake. Do you want to leave this shithole *right now*, with me, get in that badass Thunderbird out there, and run away?"

Cake doesn't know why, but he wants to cry. Like he can feel the lump in his throat, like he'd swallowed too many fries. It's just sitting there, waiting for an answer.

"Right now. We can leave."

"You're married," Cake says.

"This isn't a marriage. It's a joke."

"But your husband…"

"He's an asshole and doesn't deserve the skin he's in."

Cake's eyes break from hers. He looks at the door. Heart racing.

"Cake. Do you want to start over? I've got that car. I've got money. And darling, we can fuck like bunnies all across this desert."

Cake's eyes shoot back to this woman. This gorgeous woman who isn't quite old enough to be his mother but enough to have been his babysitter, tucking him into bed at night, where he dreams of her shapely hips grinding the innocence out of him.

"Cake?" Lucille calls from across the

diner. He can hear her, but he can't look. The vampiric embrace has him. "Cake! Come on. We got orders."

In a move so quick he shocks himself, Cake grabs the woman's arm and pulls. "Let's go."

It takes all of twenty seconds to get through the door and into the driver's seat of that badass Thunderbird.

CHAPTER 4: CONNER

Conner Sibbald washes his hands in the restroom sink, looks at himself in the mirror. He's studying wrinkles, checking his teeth, wondering why there's a tan line on his forehead and is it because he's losing his hair? He calls bullshit on that, shuts the water off, and reaches for a paper towel.

He's thinking about his wife and how she's getting out of line. It's been like this for a while now. And if he's honest with himself, he's surprised he hasn't slapped some sense into her yet, remind her who she is. She was the submissive type when they met. Or was that his doing? Now she's…independent. He doesn't like independent women, but he's never thought to wonder why. They're just not his type. Never will be.

He does, however, take a moment to think what a day it's been. He's got a delivery to make, and the bitch insisted on brunch. Now he doesn't even want it. He just wants to make the delivery. Holding this amount of cash makes him nervous, especially when it isn't his. And the more he thinks on it, the more he's convinced stopping here was a stupid fucking idea. It's time to go. The bitch can eat later.

Conner tosses the paper towel on the floor and pushes through the restroom door.

The first thing he sees is the Thunderbird pulling out. Tires raising hell, rubber turned to smoke. The first thing he thinks is: *The money!* The second: *I gotta grab the bitch and haul ass.* But when he glances at booth C and sees the bitch is gone, sees the waitress with her hands on her hips, yelling, "What in the hell?!", he puts two and two together.

Conner has ruined a handful of faces in his life, broken some limbs. But he's only ever killed one man. And with that, there was no other way out. Conner owed money, was given a job, and that job included a shotgun and a man who owed money too. A hell of a lot more money. So, it was either kill the man, or the next in line gets the shotgun and Conner eats the bullet.

Funny thing was, he never shed a tear or broke a sweat when killing the guy. Turns out the only thing stopping him from killing more is prison. He's never done a stint, and sure as hell isn't going to do a lifetime.

But prison isn't on his mind right now. It's broken legs and missing fingers. *His* broken legs and his missing fingers if he doesn't get that money back.

So, here he is again, a fork in the road. Kill or be killed. And with that dumb slut and her independence putting a taint in their love, this is killing two birds.

"Where's that kid live?" Conner is talking to the waitress with the big tits. Her jaw is slack, and she looks confused. "Hey!" Conner grabs her arm, hard.

She turns and slaps him, and he takes the whole palm, knocking him back a step.

"Okay, cunt." A second later, he has her face in his hand, pulling her toward him. "Where. Does. That. Kid. Live?"

"I can't tell you that!"

"Hey, asshole. Let go of her." It's a man sitting at the counter, the last bite of lemon meringue in his mouth.

Conner keeps his grip on the waitress, digging nails into the skin behind her jaw. But his other hand pulls a gun from inside his blazer and points it at Lemon Meringue. "I don't have time for this. Give me that kid's address or I'm putting a bullet into every person here."

A woman in a far booth yipes, grabs her toddler from the booster chair. There are four other people in the diner, but they're older than the diner itself. Arthritic knees, degenerative discs, and hearing aids, dementia on the horizon. The one man who could have done something has a 9mm barrel pointed at his chest.

Piss trickles down the waitress's legs, hits the floor, and creeps toward the counter in a golden stream. Some of the people look at it. Conner sees it and knows for sure he'll get the address.

"You got three seconds," he says.

"I...I don't know the address, but I can give you directions."

"Then do it!"

"It's on Strate Avenue. Blue house with white shutters. A big, blue house full of apartments. Three of them, I think. He lives upstairs."

"You gotta give me more than that, lady. Give me a landmark, a cross street. Somethin'."

The woman's chin dimples with fear and starts to quiver. "It's one block past Irvine. There's a convenience store across the street."

"What's the store called?"

"Dixie Mart," Lemon Meringue says.

Conner uses the gun like he's pointing a finger. "You just saved the lady's life. Now…!" he shouts. "I want everyone in that corner of the restaurant. One quick move and bullets start flying, so watch out for that piss. Slip in it, and I'll shoot ya."

Already in the corner booth, the lady and her toddler stay put, while the rest make their way. Conner switches targets every few moments, letting each person know that no one's safe. He pulls his cell out. Slides his thumb, scrolls, taps. He puts the phone to his ear. "Now nobody move."

Shasta picks up on the fourth ring.

"I need your help. I'm out on Sixty-Six at this shithole diner…yeah, that's the one.

Diane stole the car, and the trunk is full. You hear what I'm saying to you? The trunk is full…Yeah. Leave now and don't stop for nothin'. I don't care if the Pope's crossing the street at a redlight. If I go down. You're going with me."

Conner taps the phone, puts it in his pocket.

"Okay then." He eyes the cowering patrons. "Let's see if you can manage to stay alive another ten minutes."

CHAPTER 5: CAKE AND DIANE

"We gotta stop at my place." Cake's knuckles are bone-white on the Thunderbird's steering wheel. He's still wearing the greasy apron from his old life.

"For what?" Diane says, looking through the rear window.

"Clothes, money…"

"I got money. We'll buy you new clothes. That it?"

Cake thinks of his apartment, how empty it is, still looking like he just moved in. A single framed picture hangs on the wall—his mother. It's the same one in his wallet. "Where am I going?"

"Just keep driving west."

"Do you have a plan?"

"What do you mean, do I have a plan? Sweetie, we just met. My plan before this was to go home, pour a drink, and hope like hell my husband wasn't in the mood for love. Whatever the hell love is." Diane has her head resting on the seat, her gaze fixed on the flat terrain. Miles of land that look like the world ended years ago. "What is love, Cake?"

"Apparently not what you had, or you wouldn't be here with me."

"It's easy to say what love isn't, right? Love does not envy, it doesn't boast, it's not proud. It doesn't dishonor others, it's not self-seeking, it's not easily angered, it keeps no record of wrongs. Yep...definitely rules out my marriage."

"Is that a quote from a movie?"

"The bible. One of the Corinthians, I think."

"You a thumper?"

Diane laughs, reaches for a cigarette. "No, but I wish I was. Probably wouldn't be in this bind."

Cake's brow furrows, eyes on the road. "Didn't you just put yourself here?"

"This? This isn't a bind. This is adventure. I'm talking about the last six months with Conner." She's looking at Cake now, studying his face. "You've got nice eyes. They haven't seen much, have they, Cake?"

"I suppose not. Maybe that's why I'm here with you."

"You're here with me because I said we'd fuck like bunnies." She smiles. Not a seductive smile but one that's meant to embarrass and tease.

"You don't know me very well."

"I know you think about sex."

"Not as much as you might guess."

"Okay, so you're here for the adventure."

"If it has to be summed up in one word, sure. But the more we talk about it, the more I wonder if I've made a big mistake."

"You know what you'd be doing right now if you hadn't come? You'd be slaving in the back of that kitchen, wishing you would have walked out the door, living the rest of your life not knowing what could have been. And now you don't have to wonder." She cracks the window, and wind whistles through. She rolls it down, and her golden hair swirls in a cyclone of tendrils.

"So, where we going?" Cake takes a hand off the steering wheel and wipes a sweaty palm on his jeans.

"We'll keep going west for another hour or so, then grab some food since I didn't get to eat. Once we get into Nevada a ways, we'll get a motel. Lay low."

Cake looks at her. She's wearing a sundress, her tan legs sticking out from beneath, mid-thigh down. Around one leg is an anklet made of wooden beads and tiny seashells. Her feet are bare, wrapped in leather sandal straps, toes covered in nail polish. Periwinkle blue. "Don't take this the wrong way…but…you're not a prostitute, right? I mean…that guy back there isn't your pimp or anything."

"Don't take offense? No, Cake. I'm not a prostitute."

"You gotta admit, this whole thing. And then a motel, talking about having lots of sex. You're very assertive. Like scary assertive. It's intimidating."

"I'm a desperate soul. Just like you. I could sense it in you. We're both looking for a way out, and since you've got trusting eyes…" She squints one eye and puts her hand up, shapes it like a gun and points her finger at a street sign that says Route 66. "I pulled the trigger."

Cake looks at her again. The whole package. He's never met anyone like her. She's one-of-a-kind.

"And as far as being assertive. That's a new shoe I'm trying on. I was a cowering mouse up until you brought that food. Now I'm a fucking panther."

CHAPTER 6: CONNER AND SHASTA

Conner had smashed every cellphone in the diner and pulled the landline out from the wall.

As he waits for his friend to arrive, he's not sure who's more nervous, him or the group of people in the corner, huddling, crying, pissing on themselves. These people are in a lot better shape than he'll be if he doesn't get that money. The Candlemen don't just put a bullet in your head. They make you wish they would.

An El Camino with a gray primered door and a tall antenna sporting a tennis ball on top pulls into the parking lot of Skipp's Diner. The tennis ball has a smiley face on it, mocking the stress Conner is under.

"Adios, folks." He pushes the glass door open and runs for the El Camino, slowing only to rip the mocking tennis ball from the antenna and toss it.

"Hey!" Shasta says. He wears amber-colored shades, and his mustache sits on his lip like a thin, black worm, looking more like a smear of shit than hair. A cowboy hat rests on his head, covering a black mop that's slicked to his scalp with too much pomade, touching the neck of his usual turquoise and orange flannel. He owns many, but this one's his favorite. He's told Conner more than once.

"Head that way." Conner points west with the gun still in his hand. "And step on it!"

Shasta does, and gravel pelts the diner windows.

***

"What happened?" Shasta lights a cigarette, takes a hit, sets it in the ashtray. Smoke curls like ghostly fingers, bounces off the ceiling of the car and hovers.

"Get this. I stop at that grease farm back there cuz the wife says she's hungry. Never shoulda, man. And I knew that pulling in. I shoulda kept driving straight to Harrison's. It's what I always do, always have done. You don't fuck around with money like that in the car. Even you know that."

Shasta nods, lets a smile tease the corner of his mouth, then grabs the smoke and takes another hit, puts it back.

"I hit the john, and she bolts with the cook."

"The cook from the diner?"

"Believe that shit?"

"Who is he? Someone Diane knows?"

"Just some kid flippin' burgers. Couldn't keep his eyes off her."

"I think I'm missin' something."

"We was waitin' on our food. In the meantime, they're playing googly eyes. I take a piss. They take off. I can't make sense of it either, 'cept Diane's a hot piece of ass, and the kid already had a hard-on. Bitches, they've got that power, ya know?"

"I hear you." But Shasta knows what an asshole Conner is. The man doesn't know the first thing about how to treat a lady. "So, you know where this kid lives?"

"I sure do." Conner has his cellphone out, grinning at the screen. "Except, that's not where we're going."

"You stalkin' bastard. You got her phone tracked." Shasta cracks a smile.

"What if she turns her phone off?"

"You ever heard the expression, 'they've got an app for that?'"

"Yeah."

"Well…they've got an app for that. Now, keep heading west. That stupid whore is gonna wish she never met me."

CHAPTER 7: CAKE AND DIANE

They'd been driving for an hour. Mostly quiet between the two. Cake is distracted with a relenting internal debate. Mistake? Or new horizons? A door opening, another one closing. Weighing pros and cons, and finally concluding it doesn't matter anymore. He already jumped.

"It doesn't make a lot of sense to be running away together if we're not going to talk." Irritation is evident in Diane's voice as she draws a misshapen heart in the dust of the passenger-seat window.

"Yeah, you're right. It's just a lot to take in."

"You're scared."

"Sort of, yeah. I mean. It wasn't the best job in the world, but it was a job. And my apartment." He thinks of his apartment again. His empty apartment. "I guess that's not much of a loss either, but it was a stable bed."

"I mean, scared of my husband."

"Oh. Not really. Should I be?"

"I would think you'd be afraid of stealing any man's woman."

Cake chuckles. "You stole me. I didn't steal you."

"That's not how he'll see it, sweetie."

It feels awkward in the car. They have what they wanted but doing nothing with it. Two kids who've stolen a candy bar but won't eat it. Cake starts to unwrap it. No more regret.

"Let's do something. Anything." Cake realizes he's been squeezing the steering wheel the entire time. His fingers ache. He stretches them, cracks his knuckles.

"Ever had road head?" Diane has this smile on her face, like a friend just dared her to flash a passing car.

Cake looks at her, those legs. His stomach roils with barbed wire.

"Damn. You just call it out, huh?"

"Like you said, I'm assertive. So, have you?"

"No."

"Well?"

"Well, what?"

"Do I have to spell it out for you?"

"I don't want road head if that's what you're asking."

"Why? I told you we'd fuck like bunnies."

"I don't want that either."

"What. Am I too old? Is that it? I'll have you know, there isn't a single stretchmark on me, and my tits are like fucking rocks. All natural. One's a little bigger than the other, but I'll stand 'em up to any eighteen-year-old homecoming queen."

"No...you're not too old. You're perfect."

"Then what's the problem? Wait...are you gay?"

"I think we've already established I'm not."

"Then we're back to wondering why the hell you dropped everything to come with me."

Cake tightens his grip again. "Because I hate my life. I hate what I've done with it, working that shit job. Do you know what it's like staring at the same long faces while they eat the same shit food, as I flip and stir and sweat over a grill the size of a picnic table? And I left with you because you're *not* too old. And you're not too young. You're gorgeous, and I'm fucking lonely, and I want to see you naked and touch you and kiss you. But not like this. Not while you're telling me I should fear your husband. And not in your husband's car."

Diane grabs Cake's face, presses her lips to his, and gently kisses him, while he watches the road with the corner of his eye. She whispers, her breath a hot spring. "If we don't start living, this whole thing is for naught."

A rock forms in Cake's throat, and he subtly adjusts his jeans to accommodate the sudden rush of blood down below. "Is that another bible quote?" he whispers back.

Diane throws herself against the seat, head tossed back and laughing. "Not everything's a quote, Cake. Sometimes a moment births the perfect words."

"Okay, now *that* sounds like a quote."

"Just another moment, sweetie."

"Alright, so how about we start living by grabbing some food." He nods at a giant golden arch up ahead.

CHAPTER 8: CONNER AND SHASTA

"I think they stopped." Conner holds the cell in his hands, pointing at the screen with a manicured nail. "They're still on Sixty-Six." He taps the screen. "McDonald's. They're at fucking McDonald's." He laughs, and his furrowed brow lightens up. "Too easy, my friend. Too fuckin' easy."

"You gonna kill 'em?" Shasta has taken his hat off, the slicked streaks of his thinning black hair look like shiny spider legs gripping his skull. Beads of sweat mix with his mustache. The AC is dead, and Conner has already complained about it twice.

"I ain't against it. Not the kid anyway. The bitch, I haven't decided. She'll get a good fuckin', I know that much."

"She ain't wife material, Connie. Not if she's stealin' from you."

"It was a stupid thing to do, get married. Don't ever do it. Bitches are trouble."

"Shit…marriage ain't for me. I like my pussy on the side. Gotta hit the buffet. Eatin' the same course meal after meal? Fuck that."

"I hear ya." Conner smiles at the cellphone screen as the distance between him and his money shortens.

CHAPTER 9: CAKE AND DIANE

"The burgers used to be bigger." Diane takes a bite of her Big Mac, chases it down with an ice-filled Coca-Cola.

Cake shoves a fry into his mouth. "What do you mean?"

"I saw this side-by-side comparison photo once. It was of a Big Mac decades ago versus what they look like now. I think they skimp over time, real slow like so we don't notice. Like boiling a frog."

"Then they charge more, but production costs less."

"Exactly."

"Big corporations. They're the devil."

"Sure tastes heavenly, though."

"And that's how they get you." Cake tosses another fry into his mouth and winks at her. It's an innocent wink. He would have offered the same to a niece during the conversation, but somehow letting this one go feels like flirting. And how did she read it? *Looks like he wants that road head after all*. But that's not what it says. The wink is just his way of letting loose, letting the wall crumble, and leaving regret behind. Living in the moment. Living, period.

"So, how long have you been married?" Cake asks.

"Four months."

Cake nearly chokes on the fry. "Four months?"

Diane wipes her mouth with a napkin. Cake points to the other side of her mouth. She gets it. "We met two months before that."

"Okay, that makes sense. You can't get to know someone in two months. Hell, I knew a girl for…" He waves his hand. "Doesn't matter. Just takes a while is all. Sometimes years."

"Are you not talking about her because it still hurts or because you think I don't want to hear about it?"

"A little of both." Cake decides he's done with the food and tosses the fry in his hand on the tray. "But it doesn't matter. It's in the past."

Diane watches him for a while, his eyes trailing out the window, his mind elsewhere. "I wanted to be a teacher," she says. "I went to college for exactly one semester before deciding I don't even like kids. I named my first dog Eggs because it was my favorite food. Now they're not even in my top ten, and the dog ran away a month later. I only like sitcoms with laugh tracks because it makes me feel less alone and I think I need to be told when to laugh. And no matter how hot I get, I can't sleep with a fan on because then I can't hear if someone's breaking into my house."

Cake smiles, picks up the fry he'd rejected only moments before. "So…this is us getting to know each other?"

"The speed round," she smiles back, shoves the Big Mac in her mouth.

"Okay." Cake sits back, like he's preparing for something much bigger than offering trivial facts. "I wanted to be an engineer like my dad, until I found out what an asshole he was. Then I wanted to be a stripper just because I knew it'd piss him off, but I can't dance worth a shit and —"

"You're too shy," she points the hamburger at him as she says it.

"Exactly. I had three dogs…poodles…none of which were actually mine. They were my dad's, his *kids* who never disappointed him. His words, not mine."

"You're right…He is an asshole. Continue." Diane takes another bite of her burger.

"My favorite food is pizza, like a *normal* person."

"Touché."

"And I don't like sitcoms with laugh tracks because I don't like being told what to do or when to do it."

"That's quite a controversial statement coming from a diner cook who answers to Flo every day."

"Flo?"

"Waitress from a sitcom. If you didn't hate them, you'd know that."

"Lucille is the exception. She means well. And I'm no idiot. You don't get to pick and choose where you want to work when your accolades consist of a GED and a talent for flipping a hotcake without making a mess."

"You're a self-deprecator. You can add that to the list."

"What's that mean?"

"It means you under value yourself. You're a self shit-talker. Don't do that. The more you do it, the more you believe it. It's a dream killer."

"Not if you never had any dreams."

Diane's eyes go saucer-wide, as movement in the window catches her attention. "Ohh shiiiit…"

CHAPTER 10: SHASTA AND CONNER

"Pull around back." Conner is sitting up straight, gun tucked into the holster under his blazer. Heart racing. Smile plastered. "Try not to make a scene. The goal here is the money. Taking them with us is a bonus."

Shasta parks the car behind McDonald's and dons his hat. He gets out, follows Conner toward the fast-food joint.

Sweat drips from Conner's brow. Ninety degrees in a car with no AC and the stress of losing the money—the perfect recipe for a soaked shirt. But now he can hardly wait to see their faces. Daddy's home, and there's an unwanted hand in the cookie jar.

He wants to go in guns blazing, feeding bullets to the whore and the cook, but the hassle of witnesses holds him back. The Candlemen can deal with law enforcement snooping around, but he doesn't want them knowing he lost the money. Too embarrassing. And a demotion is not on his to-do list.

He sees the Thunderbird, considers just blasting a hole in the trunk and grabbing the cash, but that's the easy way out. And the bitch needs a lesson learned. "Go watch the Bird," Conner says. "I'll head inside. They come out, do what you gotta do."

CHAPTER 11: CAKE AND DIANE

"Where?" Cake stands up, looks through the window.

"He just pulled in with a friend of his. We gotta get out of here, Cake. Or we're dead."

"We're in a public place. What's he gonna do?"

Diane looks at Cake. Her eyes are two marbles, deep-blue and buried in sorrow. "I should have told you."

"Told me what?"

"This is more than a jealous husband and an unhappy wife." She grabs his hand and pulls him toward the front exit. "I'll tell you in the car."

Cake follows her lead, and the two run through the doors and into the parking lot, just about the same time Shasta makes it to the Thunderbird. Diane locks eyes with him. "Don't do this, Shasta. I'm beggin' you. You know what he'll do."

"What the fuck did you run off with the money for then?"

"It's not about the money. It's about getting away from him." Diane swings her head back, looks at the giant windows along the burger joint. She can't see through them, only a reflection of the sky.

"I can't let you leave, Diane." Shasta lifts his cowboy hat and runs fingers through the greasy spider legs. "Not with the money."

With all this talk of money, Cake realizes he's in deep. But so is Diane—a woman he feels might be worth fighting for, if only to help her escape from something dangerous. So, he balls a fist and drives it into Shasta's mustache. The man lets out a grunt and falls backward, eyes rolled, nose leaking red.

Cake still has the keys. He runs to the driver's side door, gets in. Diane's already seated. He can hear Conner's voice to his right—a boisterous grit buried in the man's throat. A guttural hacking.

"Yer gonna die, bitch!"

An explosion. Cake knows right away it's a gun going off. The bullet hits the car, but he's not sure where. Another shot. This time, glass shatters. The car's in gear, and his foot's on the gas. Floored. Tires run through bushes, spitting evergreen behind them. One more shot from the gun, and there's a dull *tink* behind them.

The car is on the road, heading west again, the speedometer buried. "Okay, let's hear it." Cake's out of breath. He'd been holding it.

"There's money in the trunk." Diane is ducked down in the seat, brushing a million glass shards out of her hair.

"Kinda gathered that. How much?"

"Half a million."

Cake swallows hard, a cold sweat creeps over his skin. "So, am I just the getaway guy? The scapegoat? Why the hell steal half a million dollars and drag me into it?"

Diane sits up and looks out the rear window, watches the miles stretch between her and the burger joint. "The money has nothing to do with it. It just happened to be there. One minute I'm listening to Conner tell me I need to act like a woman. The next, he's in the bathroom and I decide I've had enough. In hindsight, I should have waited until the money was delivered."

"Delivered? Is your husband in the mob or something?"

"The mob? No. Organized crime? Sort of, though it's not that organized if you ask me." Diane brushes the rest of the glass off her lap.

"I thought guys like that didn't tell their wives everything."

"He doesn't. Not really. But I'm no idiot, and he's not exactly quiet when his little friends are around. The math is pretty easy. Also, can we stop calling him my husband? It's over."

Cake looks at the speedometer—one hundred mph. Glances at the fuel gauge—three-quarters full. "How'd he find us?"

"Couldn't have been hard. For starters, we're still on Sixty-Six. He knows I'm starving and would stop for food at some point. But I figured an hour away was plenty. And earlier, I asked him to take me to Disney Land. He knows I've been wanting to go my whole life. Disney is west, which is where we're headed."

"Disney Land? That was your plan?"

"Not a plan, just a goal."

"Okay, we've gotta get off Sixty-Six." Cake looks in the rearview. "They can't be that far behind."

Diane faces Cake, tucks a leg under her. "You really took care of Shasta back there."

"That the guy I hit?"

"Yeah. He's Conner's right hand."

"Didn't sound like it. Sounded like he would have let you go if you begged hard enough."

"He would've for a BJ. He's got a thing for me. If there's anything that could drive a wedge between the two of them, it's me. He's always telling Conner to lay off when he gets in his moods. Sometimes I think the only reason Conner hasn't beat the shit out of me is because he'd have to hear it from his buddy."

"Sounds like Conner's got a warped code he lives by."

"What do you mean?"

"Like everything he does is okay, just so long as he doesn't hit you. A way of justifying the bullshit."

"You know…I think you're right."

Cake takes a hard right down a road that looks like it'd been started just last week—a dirt path between tumbleweeds and coyote shit. A cloud of dust kicks up behind them, and he prays that'll be gone by the time Conner gets close. He floors it.

"What's down here?" Diane watches through the window as Route 66 fades.

"Nothin'. Just need to get off that damn road before we both take a bullet through the headrest. You got a smoke?"

"Yeah…You one of them who just starts and stops smoking whenever you feel like it?" Diane fishes through her tiny purse for a pack of Winstons.

"Told myself a long time ago I'd never be a slave to anything."

She pulls a smoke from the pack, lights it, hands it over. "Except for a job flipping burgers."

She's right. He was stuck where he didn't want to be. Powerless to a paycheck that barely kept him out of a dumpster, hunting for food. "I mean drugs, booze…women. All the shit people find themselves depending on."

Diane laughs. "The hell do you call this then? A car full of money and a hot piece of ass by your side, neither of which you know the first thing about. But here you are. Jobless and running for your life for 'em."

Cake takes a small hit from the cigarette, lets his lungs remember what it's like. "You ever consider I'm just a nice guy who saw a woman in need?"

Diane laughs harder this time. It's exaggerated. "Now we're back to you not making a move until I mentioned sex."

"Wasn't my motivator. That ain't me."

"Well, aren't you a rare breed?"

Cake keeps his eyes on the road ahead. "I like to think so."

CHAPTER 12: SHASTA AND CONNER

Conner kicks Shasta's car for the third time. They're on the side of Route 66, ten miles from McDonald's. The hood is popped, and smoke pours from the radiator.

"A cook and a gallon of coolant," Conner says. "That's all it took to get my nuts in a vice. You gotta be fuckin' kidding me."

"She's still tracked, right?" Shasta puffs on a smoke before flicking it into the road.

Conner looks at his phone, runs a hand through sweaty hair. "Yeah."

"Then you've got nothing to worry about. No matter how far they get, you'll have 'em. We just need to get this baby fixed, then we'll make a road trip of it."

Conner looks up, eyes drilling holes through Shasta. "This ain't no vacation, cockface. And fuck your car. We're calling a cab, or hitching, or running our asses off to the nearest town and renting one. And you're paying for it. Who doesn't use coolant in fucking Texas?"

"Must be a leak."

"Fuck this. I'm callin' Jones. Shoulda called him to begin with." Conner pushes numbers on his phone.

"Aww shit, Connie. Don't call that asshole. Damn redneck nearly got me killed last year, callin' that black boy in the bar a coon. Two seconds later, the place lights up with white eyes and gritting teeth. They came outta the woodwork."

"Well, you lived didn't you?" Puts the phone to his ear.

"Not without some scars up here." Shasta points to his head. "And I like blacks. They sing good, play good, too. Ever hear Stanley Clarke? Fusion. Plays a mean—"

"Shut the fuck up, Shasta. I don't give a shit whether you like Jessie Jackson or Christopher Columbus."

"Christopher Columbus?"

Conner puts a finger up, shushing Shasta. "Hey, Jones! How ya doin', man? Listen, you up for a road trip?...Northwest, maybe as far as Oklahoma. Maybe New Mexico...Nah, it ain't that. Something else...There's a grand in it for ya...great! How soon can you get to..." Conner looks around, sees an old, abandoned gas station. "We're on Sixty-Six, about ten miles west of McDonald's, sittin' outside an old Exxon...Just Shasta and me. Aww come on, Jones. How about two grand, and we'll tape Shasta's mouth shut."

"Tape *his* mouth shut, racist dick." Shasta says.

"Okay, how soon?...three hours!?...the hell you doin' in Nacogdoches?...a convention?...Books? Leave right now, and I'll give you three thousand, but that's it. Okay...Yeah, ten miles past McDonald's. We're here on the side of the road. Shasta doesn't know what coolant is."

"I know what the fuck coolant is," Shasta says. "I'm tellin' ya, I got a leak."

Conner hangs the phone up. "Three fuckin' hours. He's at a book convention, meeting authors. Who the fuck wants to meet an author?"

Shasta scratches his head. "Depends on the author, I suppose. I'd meet the hell outta Lovecraft."

"Now there's a racist for ya."

"Bullshit."

"I don't even know who the fuck Lovecraft is, dumbass. But with a name like that, I can tell she writes romance."

CHAPTER 13: CAKE AND DIANE

After a few more turns, they're heading west, though keeping clear of Sixty-Six. Diane has her feet on the dash. "So, tell me about your first love."

"That came out of nowhere."

"I'm curious. And I love a good romance."

"Aren't they supposed to have happy endings?" Cake says.

"Tell me anyway."

"Okay…Her name was Marianne."

"I've always loved that name. I hate mine. It's a secretary's name, or a real estate agent. Someone with a stick up their ass."

"I don't like mine either."

"Is that why you go by Cake?"

He chuckles. "That is my real name."

"You're not serious."

"My grandmother was a cake decorator, kind of a mini celebrity within a hundred-mile radius. Owned her own business. And my mother, she worshipped her. So, when my grandmother died, my mom had a breakdown, nearly had a miscarriage. She wasn't in the right state of mind when she had me, but by the time she was, the name stuck."

"Wow." Diane picked at the polish on her toes. Periwinkle Blue. "Good thing your grandmother wasn't into pies. Doesn't quite have the same ring to it."

"Funny."

"So…Marianne."

"Typical story, really. High school sweethearts and all that. Inseparable. She was homecoming queen, then she got a scholarship and left. The end."

"She left you for college?"

"Probably the best decision she's ever made."

"Why would you say that? You loved her, right?"

"More than you can imagine. But look at me. Four years later, and all I've got to offer is a job any teenager who knows how to hold a spatula could get."

Diane shifts in her seat, sits sideways, facing Cake. "It's because you settled. She broke your heart, and you never got over it. You would have thrived with her. It's like a dog at the pound. Inside that cage, they're not themselves. Their tail's between their legs, sleeping all day, depressed. But you bring one home, and it's a whole different creature. They thrive. They live. You've been in a cage, Cake. And Marianne put you there when she decided a career is more important than love."

"You make it sound so poetic."

"That's because love *is* poetic. It's the origin of all things poetic. Ever read Song of Solomon?"

Cake laughs. "From the bible?"

"Yeah, from the bible. It's beautiful. Check it out some time." Diane digs through her purse for gum, pulls out two sticks and hands one to Cake. Big Red. "So, that was your first love. You're old enough to have at least another."

Cake pops the gum in his mouth, chews. "Yeah, you're right. With the other, I thought it was love but still not sure."

"Let me guess. She was gorgeous and incredible in bed, but maybe that's all there was."

"Right again." He lets his foot off the gas, eyes a crossroad up ahead.

"Yeah, those are tough. Can't tell if it's infatuation or actual love. Personally, I think if you have to ask, then it's lust disguised, which fades away before you know it."

"Sounds like you've been there."

"A few times. So…what was so special about the sex?"

Cake glances at her. "Uhh…"

"Don't be shy." Diane takes her sunglasses that'd been resting on her head and drops them onto the bridge of her nose, sultry eyes peeking over them. "She give good head? Know how to move her hips just right?"

Cake stops the car at the crossroads, looks left, then right and catches Diane's eyes.

"She sucked it real good, huh?"

Something about the way she says it, the way her lids go heavy, and how her fingers grab the seat when the words come out. He wants her. He's wanted her ever since that first smile, but he'd put up a wall he couldn't tear down. It's because he likes her. He likes her enough to say no, to make sure this is what she really wants too, instead of playing the role she's played for years—a slick hole to offer because it's how she sees herself. An automaton fulfilling the function she's been programmed to do, with the hope it fills a void she has. It's all she knows.

Diane leans over, buries her head in his crotch, quickly finds his zipper. But he grabs the back of her head, pulls her by the hair. Not hard, just enough to send the message. "Don't," he says.

She slaps him, then curls up in the seat against the door, pouting, eyes on the North Texas wasteland. The two sit in silence for the next few moments. Cake can feel her shame, the embarrassment. He turns the car left.

"You're better than that," he says.

She stares off, eyes glaze over with tears.

Cake thinks he's figured her out. She's been conditioned. While there may have been a time where she dreamt of ponies and white-picket fences, a knight in shining armor and a big wedding, blonde-haired and blue-eyed kids who cling to her legs when scared, somewhere along the way life showed its ugly face, and she caved. Bending over got her where she thought she needed to go. It wasn't about finding love anymore. It was about surviving. A string of bad men painting a different picture, where needs are met as long as legs are spread, and self-worth was a lie— a three-legged horse you could never put your money on.

While she stews in her shame, the clock on the dash reads 2:30. The clouds up ahead promise a storm. A different storm behind them altogether.

"Do you wanna give up? Turn the car around and go home?" Cake says.

"That's not an option."

"You said he doesn't hit you. You could give him the car, the money, and leave."

"Yet. He hasn't hit me yet. He'll use me as an example of what happens when you cross Conner Sibbald." She says his name like it tastes bad on her tongue.

"But you're his wife."

She sighs and pinches the bridge of

her nose. "Were you not there when bullets were flying? You think I'm afraid of a black eye after that? What Conner and I have, who he is. It's out of a fuckin' movie. Whatever predictable plot you can come up with dealing with a character like him, it's dead on." She looks at Cake. "Why? Do you want to give up?"

"No. I wouldn't have left in the first place if I didn't plan on going the distance." It's a lie. The minute they pulled out of the diner parking lot, he questioned the decision and wished he could turn back. The money, the chase, and now the threat of losing their lives, it's not what he expected. Not what he signed up for. But they crossed the point of no return miles ago.

Silence between them for miles. Clouds clashing, darkening the sky. Dust kicking as they head north. Roadkill waves from the side of the road like a sign of things to come.

CHAPTER 14: SHASTA, CONNER, AND JONES

Conner has had just about enough of Shasta by the time Jones pulls up. He's spent the last three hours listening to his friend speak on everything from the current political climate to his favorite sex positions. Turns out, Shasta is a foot man, something Conner never understood, dirty toes in your mouth.

Jones is sixty years old and built like a bull, brown skin and bald. He served in the Iraq War and was sent home with a pair of boots, a single medal, a bad case of PTSD, and a grudge toward the US. He hates America and vows to move to Mexico one day. So far, that day hasn't come, but talking about it is still a favorite pastime.

For fifteen years, he was a bodyguard in the organization Conner later found himself in but has since retired due to a run-in with two German shepherds.

One hundred and forty-three stitches later, Jones developed a limp, an addiction to pain pills, and an intense fear of canines. When he got home from the hospital, he shot his dog in the backyard, then doused him in gasoline, and threw the match. Now Conner reveres him and his unpredictable nature. And damn does the guy get shit done.

Jones looks straight ahead while Shasta hops in the back, Conner in the front. Conner says, "Appreciate it, Jones. Sorry we interrupted your book thing."

"Yep," Jones says. He looks in the rearview mirror, see's Shasta with a cigarette. "No smoking."

Shasta rolls his eyes and flicks his smoke into the wind.

Jones pulls his foot off the brake, and they set off. "Where's the money?" He's got his hand out, waiting for delivery.

"Money's in my car, which is where we're headed."

"And where is that exactly?"

Conner looks at his phone, taps the screen a few times. "Harperton."

"Harperton? Where the heck's that?"

Jones says.

"Just outside Bodenville."

"Bodenville? How far you think three thousand bucks stretches, huh?"

"I'll throw in a full tank and dinner."

"No fast food either," Shasta says from the backseat.

"Shut the fuck up, Shasta."

Jones swings a giant, back-handed fist, and belts Conner in the chest. Air leaves his body in a breathy squeal. It's in that moment he remembers Jones' disdain for profanity in his car and makes a mental note to watch his mouth. The big Hispanic is a loose wheel, and taking a spontaneous fist or two is something not uncommon when in the company of the brown bull.

"Sorry, Jones. It's been one of them days."

"They say Hitler was a jew," Shasta spits randomly. "And gay."

Conner catches Jones looking in the rearview, eyes squinting. If the car stops and Jones throws his friend from it, he won't be surprised.

"So, this convention." Conner pours some water on the fire. "What kind of books they got there? You read them westerns, right?"

"I read everything I can get my hands on. Westerns, thrillers, some fantasy if I'm feelin' it. Bought myself ten new books at the con, got a few signed."

"Never been much of a reader myself," Conner says.

"You don't say."

"I prefer celluloid. Love me the visuals of a good story."

"Well, that *celluloid* you enjoy is often based on a book. A book that's better than those visuals you love. And the ones that aren't, they're still written by writers. You oughta do yourself a favor and crack the spine of a good read now and then. Might even broaden your vocabulary beyond piss, fuck, and shit."

Conner wants to put a bullet in the man, see his condescending brain squeeze right through the driver's side window. He never really liked him, but the desperate call was for two reasons. One being the obvious ride needed to get where they were going. The other was the muscle. If shit went down, he knew he could count on

Jones, like him or not.

"Ever read Mein Kampf?" Shasta says.

"You think I don't know you're mocking me, boy?"

"Just makin' conversation is all."

"Jones…tell us about the time you took care of Rochester." Conner has to do something, or these two in the car together on a road trip isn't going to end well. The tension needs breaking, and no better way than to give Jones the floor, reciting one of his own prideful stories. If there is one thing the man loves more than reading, it's telling his own stories that highlight his flex. Rochester is one of those stories.

"Rochester. Now there's a man who wishes he ain't ever been born." Jones chuckles. "I was guarding for Juarez at the time, and Juarez, he had this sweet piece of ass named Candy. Her real name was Denise, but he called her Candy, and she seemed to like it. So, Juarez and Candy, they're invited to a party on Mulholland Drive. If you've been to Angeles, you know what I'm talking about, but Shasta there, I don't think he has. Mulholland is this windy road full of money. Directors, actors, screenwriters. They got all the real estate up there. So, I'm driving Juarez and his lady up there, and they spend the evening dancin', doin' lines, gabbin', until Candy disappears. Juar has me looking all over this fourteen-bedroom house for her. I never seen so many bathrooms."

Jones pulls a package of cinnamon flavored toothpicks from his shirt pocket and puts one in his mouth. "So, ten minutes go by, and I find Candy in a laundry room the size of a two-car garage. Total waste of space, that room. And right there against the wall is Candy, sitting on the washer, with a man's head between her legs, her nails deep into his afro. He wasn't even black, neither. He just thought it was 1979. That's Rochester. So, the washer's rocking, Candy's head is thrown back, eyes closed. She doesn't even know I'm there.

"Now, I'm thinkin' all kinds of ways to handle this. I should mention, Juarez treated me good. Real good. He treated Candy good, too. So, no way in heck was I gonna let this beaver-munchin' backstabber off easy. Seeing her get off like that, by another man. It hurt, knowing I'd have to go to Juar and tell him his Candy ain't so sweet.

"You didn't hurt *her*, did you?" Shasta says.

Jones looks in the rearview. "I'll let you be the judge of that. So, this guy's goin' to town, lappin' it up, and I walk up behind him and say, 'How's the candy taste?' He pulls back, and I slam Candy's knees together, right over his ears. They pop, and blood pours."

"Damn!" Shasta says, and Conner gives him a cautious eye that says, *Don't be swearing in this car.* "I mean…daaaang. So, did you break her knees?"

"Nah, but she couldn't walk right for a month."

"What about Rochester?"

"He can still hear out of one ear, if he's got his hearing aid in and the wind's just right."

"What was plan B?" Shasta says. "You said you were thinkin' of all kinds of ways."

"Stuff him in the washer 'til he fit."

CHAPTER 15: CAKE AND DIANE

Diane is sleeping, head resting on the window. Without her conversation, it gives Cake too much time to think. Regret is in the rearview. It's on the road ahead. Out every window. He wonders if fucking like bunnies really was the catalyst for motivation. Not so much the act itself but just hearing the words from the mouth of a beautiful woman. Spontaneous and unpredictable. The words triggered excitement and the thought of adventure. But it wasn't long before that quest for love and poetic chaos turned to a dangerous game of survival.

He can't stop asking himself about the endgame, the best-case scenario. Did they really think this would end in a happily ever after? That her husband would just give up his pursuit, and they'd live at Disney Land, heavy petting in the teacups, screwing in the flower gardens, and wiping their asses with one-hundred-dollar bills?

The past hundred miles have been spent heading west in a zig-zag pattern, like a deer through the woods, trying to lose the hunter. Despite thinking it's not the best idea, he is heading to Disney Land. No sense in Diane risking all if there's no reward at the end. She deserves it.

Curiously, all the talk of Marianne put her in his mind, where she hasn't been for nearly half a year now. He still loves her, probably always will, but not much time is spent reflecting on the memories they'd made. To Cake, that makes about as much sense as window shopping. You know you're not bringing it home, so why pretend?

But on this quiet road trip with a sleeping stranger, he finds himself entertaining thoughts he hasn't allowed for months, like the time they grilled burgers in the park. The worst they'd ever had, with half the meat seeping through the grate, sizzling on the charcoal. The smell was divine, the taste was not. They celebrated the bad meal with a quickie. The dress she'd worn made it easy, as she sat on his lap while they kissed tenderly.

Diane stirs awake, rubs the sleep from her eyes and reaches for her purse. Lights up a smoke and offers one to Cake. He declines. She cracks the window, and the smoke trails out in thin wisps.

She looks at her phone, forgetting she'd turned it off after they left the diner. She looks at the dashboard. "Is that the right time?"

"Should be. We're still in Texas."

"Damn. Figured we'd be in New Mexico by now. We still heading west?"

"That's where Disney Land is, right?" Cake looks at her and smiles. She smiles back. She's gorgeous, and Conner is a fool.

CHAPTER 16: SHASTA, CONNER, AND JONES

"When we hit Bodenville and get to your car, we're grabbing dinner," Jones says.

Conner swallows hard and checks his phone to see exactly where his wife is now. "The car's not in Bodenville anymore."

Jones checks the rearview, then slams on the brakes. Tires scar the road and scream to a stop. "I get the sense you're leaving out some details, Connie."

"Shiiiit," Shasta says.

Jones swings his arm around, and his fist just misses Shasta's nose. "You keep the car clean. I don't wanna hear your expletives. One more time and you're walkin' back. You hear me?"

"Dang, Jones. Take it down a notch," Shasta says. "Can't smoke, can't swear. I'm like a kid stuck behind his parents back here."

"Then hit the road." Jones' eyes are

stuck to Shasta's—two lasers burning holes in his head.

Shasta crosses his arms and looks out the window.

Jones peels his eyes off Shasta and glues them to Conner. "So…are we on a wild goose chase for this money of yours? Is that it?"

Conner hates being in the position where he's mouse-sized, hates it even more that Shasta's in the audience. "Yes and no. Diane took the car. It's got money in the trunk, three thousand of that being yours. Thing is, I've got her tracked." Conner holds up his cell phone, shakes it.

"Who's Diane?"

"Broad I married earlier this year."

"You got married? *You*?"

"What can I say. I thought she was the one. Turns out she's nothing but a thief."

"Five grand, or you can get out and walk too." Jones takes his toothpick out, sets it in the sparkling clean ashtray.

"We agreed on three. Plus dinner, and I'm covering gas. I think that's pretty fair, Jones."

"What's fair is telling me what I'm

getting into. You're lucky I don't kick your butt out right now in the middle of nowhere."

Conner looks around at the tumbleweeds, beaming sun, and stretch of endless road. "Alright. Five grand, but you can buy your own dinner."

"Total BS, Conner," Shasta says. "You didn't have to wait three hours for me. I came running right away to save your as.....butt."

"And if it weren't for you and your no coolant, I wouldn't be forking over five k for another ride."

"He's right, ya know," Jones says to the rearview.

Shasta's arms fold tighter, like he's hugging himself.

Jones grabs another toothpick and lets his foot off the brake.

CHAPTER 17: CAKE AND DIANE

Cake tells Diane they're stopping for gas and some snacks. He's been waiting for a station with lots of traffic, where if someone came asking questions, the cashier would have a hard time remembering all the faces they'd seen that shift.

"Do me a favor," he says. "Duck down in the seat. If Conner somehow finds his way here and starts asking questions, I don't want anyone to have seen you. I'm not sure he got a good look at me, so offering a description will be harder. But you…it's hard to miss you."

She smiles and bats her eyes playfully, then moves the seat back and fits herself on the floorboard, arms on the seat, hand under chin, looking up at Cake. "You got a nice jawline, Cake."

He smiles, says thanks. "Any particular snack you want? Some chips?

Beef jerky? Soda?"

"Yeah, give me a bag of potato chips… a big bag. And a Diet Coke…oh, and another pack of Big Red."

"You got it." Cake puts the car in park, then hops out. "Ohh…huh, this is embarrassing, being our first date and all, but I'll need some money."

Diane chuckles and goes for her purse, pulls out six twenties. "Didn't your momma ever teach you chivalry?" She winks.

He winks back, then fills the tank with gas and heads into the store. The crisp air through the door is something he doesn't realize he's missed until it hits him. There are at least four other customers inside, another few pumping gas. He finds a big bag of Lays, the Diet Coke and grabs himself some Munchos and a Snickers, along with two waters. While at the counter, he grabs the gum and a pack of Winstons.

Like in the movies, he expects to see his face on the front page of the paper, or plastered on a TV screen, as the clerk puts two and two together. But legally he's done nothing wrong, and Conner certainly isn't going to the police. He'll handle it himself. A much less pleasant scenario.

When he gets to the car, Diane is still on the floorboard, waiting patiently. He puts the food in the backseat, gets in. He jokes about how nonthreatening she looks down there, and she playfully barks at him to hurry up and get them the hell out of there.

On the road, chips and sodas are opened, and they chow down like two kids at a sleepover, paying no mind to the mess they're making.

"We'll need a hotel soon," Cake says. "Got a preference?"

"Do you mean a two star or a five?"

"Yeah…or somewhere in between."

"Fuck it," she says. "Let's indulge. We'll stay at the nicest place we can find."

"Gonna dip into the trunk savings, huh?"

"Why not?" she says. "And at least a five-star will have security."

"Good thinking. See what you can find on your phone."

Diane hesitates, knowing when she

turns the thing on it'll be loaded with notifications from Conner. Her stomach goes sour, and she loses her appetite, closes the bag of chips.

Sure enough, when the phone starts up, there's ten missed calls from Conner and walls of threatening texts. She blocks his number.

"Check it out," Cake says, pointing up ahead to a sign that reads *Welcome to New Mexico*. "How far is Santa Fe? I think we just left Glenrio."

Diane works her phone until she gets the answer. "About three hours."

"You got three hours left in you? Not sure we can find a five-star between here and there."

"Damn…"

"Or we can settle."

"No…I didn't start this mess to sleep in a bed full of stains. It'll be worth the wait. But can we put some music on?"

Cake works the radio until a song comes on they both start singing along to.

CHAPTER 18: SHASTA, CONNER, AND JONES

Conner stares at his phone. He doesn't tell Jones the money is now outside Texas. He just shuts the screen off and tells him to keep heading straight, hoping no questions are asked.

Shasta suggests they stop to stretch their legs and take a piss. Jones agrees. He also mentions food. A tall Denny's sign touches the clouds like a giant, yellow kaiju. "That'll do," he says.

"Maybe we should eat on the run," Conner says.

"You think I'm letting you eat in Priscilla?"

Neither Shasta nor Conner has ever actually heard the name Jones had given his car, but it surprises no one.

They pull off the exit and park at Denny's. Jones shifts in his seat, puts his large, brown arm across the back of it. "Okay...don't order nothing that takes forever to cook. You get some pancakes or toast and eggs."

"What if they're not serving breakfast," Shasta says.

"It's a Denny's. They're serving breakfast. And no milk. Get water."

"How the hell...heck are you gonna tell me what to eat and drink?" Shasta in the backseat.

"Because we're pressed for time. It's quicker to get water than it is coffee or milk."

"Well, if that ain't splittin' hairs. Why the heck don't we just hit a drive-thru. You think I'm gonna sit back here stuffin' French fries in between your seats? The food's goin' in my mouth, Jones. Every bit of it."

Like before, Conner has to break the tension. "We need to stretch our legs anyway, Shasta. Just like you said. Otherwise, someone's gonna go Jack Torrance up in here."

"Fine. Now, get out so I can." Shasta pushes on the back of the passenger seat.

The two men in front get out, stretch

their backs, their arms. Shasta gets out behind them. Once he's out of the car, he says, "Can I swear now, or will *Priscilla* still get offended?"

"If talkin' like a school kid gets you off, go for it."

"Fuuuck this!" Shasta lights a cigarette and storms off toward Denny's.

Conner can't help but shake his head and chuckle but kills it quick after seeing Jones is not amused.

All three men order pancakes and water, and Shasta starts bitching. "Who the hell eats pancakes without milk?"

"I'm a little shocked you've survived as long as you have in this business," Jones says. "I'll bet you complain about your own farts too."

This time Conner doesn't hide his laughter.

"That ain't fair. I'm in the middle of this shitstorm for trying to be a good friend. My car breaks down. I'm forced to sit in the backseat with my knees to my chin, can't smoke, can't fuckin' cuss, can't order milk cuz Lord help us all if it takes an extra minute, yet we can't hit a drive-thru cuz you think we're gonna have a fucking food fight in your precious Mustang. And to top it off, you're getting five thousand dollars for sitting behind the wheel. Fuck yes, I'm complaining."

Jones just watches him, amused. "You done?"

Shasta's nostrils flare. "I'm gonna have another smoke." He slams a hand on the table and leaves the booth, heads outside.

"Connie, you've got horrible taste in friends *and* women."

"Can't argue there."

CHAPTER 19: CAKE AND DIANE

They're sitting in the parking lot of the Loretto Inn, the massive adobe structure illuminating the two in their amber lights. Cake has never seen anything like it, and feels the wall crumbling, daring himself to live in the moment. Maybe everything has led to this unforgettable night. A beautiful woman, a trunk full of money, a heart that finally beats again. And even if it all ends tonight, maybe it was worth it.

They exit the car and stretch their legs in the amber glow, thirty feet from a five-star paradise, where Diane called ahead and reserved their room—the best they had available.

"First thing tomorrow, let's ditch the car and get a new one," Diane says.

"Seriously?"

"Seems logical to me."

Cake laughs. "Ever seen the movie

Psycho?"

"About the guy who kills girls in the shower?"

"Well, he kills one girl, but yeah. Do you know how that movie starts? The woman in the shower, she steals a bunch of money, splits town, ditches her car and buys another."

"That's some unbalanced karma."

"And every move you've made is paving the way for it."

"That's ridiculous...and superstitious."

"Probably. I just don't want to see you, or me, at the bottom of a swamp."

"Then we'll throw a curveball, and we won't take showers." She smiles when she says it.

Except for a bellhop, two women at the desk, and a man on his phone sitting in one of the six overstuffed chairs, the lobby is empty. It's late.

Diane gives her name at the desk, and they're given their key on the third floor. They'd already discussed whether or not to get two rooms. Neither of them feels comfortable being apart, given the circumstances.

Cake starts to wonder if they should have parked somewhere else and walked to the hotel just to be safe but strikes the thought up as paranoia, considering the only way Conner could have possibly found out where they are is if he'd been following close behind, and there were many long stretches of road in the last several hours where no car was behind them for miles.

The ride in the elevator up to their room is silent and tense. Cake assumes it's because they're alone in a small area, heading up to spend the night together, even though there are no plans for a night of sex.

Diane finally breaks the silence as the elevator passes the second floor. "You hungry?"

"Famished. A bag of chips doesn't exactly fill you up."

"We'll get room service. Whatever you want."

Ever since the gas station, Cake has felt uncomfortable about taking her money, like she's some sugar momma. But he doesn't argue about who will pay what.

Except for the small savings he has stashed at home—which he'd actually forgotten about until now—she knows he's broke.

The elevator dings, and the door opens. A housekeeper pushes a cart by, and Cake can smell the linens and disinfectant. He steps aside against the open door and lets Diane exit first. They search the hall and follow the ascending numbers up to 307, at the end of the hall.

The room lights up when they enter, and it smells of sandalwood and linen. The ceilings are high, crossed with oak beams, the windows tall, four of which overlook a courtyard with a fountain in the center. A woman sits on a bench in front of the fountain, an e-reader in her hand. Cake counts four life-sized patinaed sculptures in the courtyard, all of them women dressed in robes striking various poses. Topiary is underlit with soft lights, and pebbles form paths among them. To the right is another wing of the hotel. All but two of the rooms are dark. One has the drapes drawn, the other open, with a couple sitting at a table, eating.

"Look at that view, Cake."

"Kinda makes you wish you could live right there in the middle of it, huh?"

"It's funny how you never know how bad you want something until you see it for the first time."

Cake has only ever seen a five-star in film, he wasn't sure what to expect, but stepping into what is essentially a luxury apartment, exceeds his expectations. The first thing he does is kick off his shoes and lay out on one of two couches.

"There's a menu here." Diane holds up a satin-covered book filled with a handful of laminated pages. "Did you have anything in mind?"

"Would it be crazy of me to order a burger and fries?"

"Yes…I won't allow it. We're getting something exotic and costly." She eyes the menu, flipping through the pages. "And a bottle of wine…I can't stand champagne. I don't get how anyone can."

"I think it's one of those things where it's tradition, so it feels like a must have for celebratory purpose. This occasion calls for it, but we're free thinkers. Red goes well with cheeseburgers."

"We're not getting cheeseburgers." She eyes him. "You want a cheeseburger because you think it's the cheapest thing on here, don't you?"

He wants to lie, but his smile gives him away. "I've gotta admit, this whole thing is odd for me. You joked about chivalry earlier, but I've got it in me. It's just hard to show given the circumstances."

"Just don't think of it as my money. This is Conner paying his dues for being an asshole. And I'm not the only one he's ruined."

Cake sits up. "You consider yourself ruined?"

Diane sits down next to him and slips her sandals off. Those beautiful periwinkle toes. "Maybe not ruined, but meeting him definitely put me on the wrong detour. Six months may not seem like a long time, but a lot can happen in half a year. Hell, look at what happened in just one day."

"Well, if it helps, not only do I not consider you ruined, I think you're wiser and your future brighter than it was yesterday. Every time we end a relationship, we learn more about ourselves, and not just about what we want but what we need. You know a hell of a lot more about both than you did six months ago."

"For your age, you're pretty wise yourself."

"You're not that much older."

She smiles, and her eyes light up. "Old enough to have been your babysitter."

For the next few moments, neither of them says a thing. They're lost in the hypnotizing gaze that comes before every first kiss. And before either of them lets anything change the moment, they submit to the pull. Cake hasn't felt the fleshy velvet of a woman's tongue in at least six months. The last time was at a bar, where he'd stopped it mid kiss, realizing it was the beer that caused the locking lips and wanted nothing to do with waking up with a stranger, only to pretend he'll call when he knew he never would.

Diane's hair feels softer than he'd thought it would, her touch more passionate and desperate. This wasn't her doing what she felt another guy wanted. This was her succumbing to her own genuine desire. It was real.

As promised, her breasts were supple with no give, natural, just another reminder they were closer in age than the numbers would have them believe. They made love on the couch, her riding him while they both glanced at the courtyard below, like it was some pornographic greenery helping get them off—a slice of paradise adding to the euphoria they created between them.

The way she grinded her hips and gazed at him while coming, reminded Cake of Marianne. And for one scary moment, he felt like he could fall in love if he wasn't careful.

CHAPTER 20: CAKE AND DIANE

They spend the evening in bed, naked and surrounded by expensive food they only eat half of. But the bottle of wine they finish. Cake smiles at the periwinkle toes peeking out from under the sheet and thinks to himself they could be the feet of a twenty-year-old. Soft, tan, and spotless. They're perfect.

They'd made love a second time while waiting for room service. Now, with bellies full of food and stirred sheets, they talk about goals and dreams, old and new. Diane mentions her love for art and surprises Cake with pictures on her phone of paintings she'd done.

"I'd love to have my own studio, just to have a space where it's cluttered with brushes and palettes and easels and way too many paints. I want to learn to stretch my own canvas and do giant paintings that cover half the wall." This is the happiest Cake has seen her since they met. This is the real her, and he loves every moment. She brings a silly side out in him, as they joke about television shows and stereotypes, cliché librarians, and their annoyance at people who wear sunglasses at night.

"What have you always wanted to do, Cake? Even if it's something that seems impossible." She brushes her feet against his leg and caresses the small patch of hair on his chest, looking into his eyes, waiting for an answer.

"Promise not to laugh?"

"Promise." She grabs his hand and folds her fingers in his.

"A country singer."

She does laugh. "I'm sorry. I'm only laughing because it's absurd to think I'd laugh about it. Why would you think that?"

"Because I don't even like country music."

Diane laughs harder now, and Cake joins her. "Then why in the world would you want to be a country singer?"

"I like the aesthetic. The cowboy hat, the flannel, the boots."

"Well then just do your thing but wear a cowboy hat, a flannel, and boots."

Cake thinks a moment, then laughs again. "Never thought of that."

"What about guitar. Can you play?"

"Nah...always wanted to learn, though."

"It's never too late to start. We'll get you one tomorrow. An acoustic, it'll match the look you're going for."

"No way. If I get one, it'll be with my own money."

"You're adorable." She slides up and kisses his neck, then meets his mouth, while her hand travels under the sheets. "It's a good thing you *are* younger, so you can keep up."

Cake grabs her face and kisses her deep and full, as she climbs on top of him for another round.

CHAPTER 21: CAKE AND DIANE

Exhausted from love, wine, and the crash of adrenaline that'd ran all day, the two sleep in the light of the moon, broken into strips by the Venetian blinds. The windows are open, allowing a breeze to caress their bare skin, letting the trickle of the fountain in the courtyard lull them to sleep, while Conner looms over them with a loaded gun.

Shasta sits on a couch, and Jones stands guard in the hallway.

Conner fumes seeing his wife lay there naked with another man, and once again made worse by Shasta as a voyeur. He thinks of the story Jones told, of smashing Rochester's head between the knees of a woman and how he took a moment to concoct the best plan. But Conner can't do that. He has no patience, not with his wife's leg wrapped around another man.

He swings the butt of his gun,

cracking the sleeping man in the head. Skin splits and blood trickles. Conner grabs him by the hair and pulls him off the bed. Diane wakes, then screams at the revelation that they've been caught and this is the beginning of the end.

As Conner pistol whips the adulterer again, keeping a fist full of hair, Diane kicks at him. "Conner!...Stop!"

"Get the bitch!" Conner says to Shasta.

Shasta grabs Diane, wraps his arms around her, purposefully groping her breasts, the only chance he'll ever have of fulfilling a fantasy he's had since he met his friend's new wife earlier that year.

He keeps an arm around her neck, with his hand cupping a breast, as though it's the only possible way to detain her. Conner takes note but says nothing. He's too busy with the bleeding man, forcing him onto the bed with the gun pointed at him.

Shasta moves out of his way, guiding Diane with him. As he stands behind her, his crotch pressed against her bare ass, he starts to grow hard and slides a hand down her backside—a lightning-quick finger down the crack of her ass and into the first hole he finds.

She jumps at the violation. "Get your fuckin' hands off me, you piece of shit!"

Conner looks, takes note again. He'll deal with it later. "Let her go, Shasta." Reluctantly, Shasta does. "Now, get some fuckin' clothes on, slut!"

"Leave him alone, Conner. He didn't do anything. I'm the one who took the money," Diane says.

Conner swings the gun again and breaks the man's nose. Blood sprays, and he falls off the bed, lifeless.

"Conner!"

"Want me to shut her up, Connie?" Shasta asks.

Conner's eyes turn to slits. "I can handle it." He reaches for her, grabs her by the arm and backhands her across the face. "I said get your fuckin' clothes on!"

"Woah, woah, woah, Connie." Shasta steps forward to intervene.

"Don't test me, man, or I'll slap the shit out of you too. Better yet, I'll have Jonesy do it." He looks back to his wife, tightens his grip on her arm until she squeals. "Shut your mouth, or I'll knock your teeth out."

Shasta deflates onto the couch and secretly smells the finger he put inside Diane.

Diane looks around the room, spots her dress and bra on the floor in front of the couch. Her panties are elsewhere. In the panic, she can't find them. Shasta sees them dangling on the corner of the couch but says nothing.

"Just take the money and the car and leave, Conner. We weren't meant for each other. It was over months ago, and you know it."

"It's over when I say it is. Now, let's go." He pulls her again, and she throws the dress over her head as they head for the door. Conner turns back to Shasta. "Beat the brains out of him and leave him for dead. But hurry up. We'll be outside."

They leave the room and shut the door. Jones is standing there, looks at Diane. "Good taste, bad judgment."

***

Shasta scrambles for the panties first and stuffs them in his pocket. He looks down at Cake. "Boy did you fuck up." Shasta kicks him four times in the side and twice in the head. Cake doesn't move, only bleeds.

***

Outside, Jones escorts Conner and his wife to the Thunderbird. Conner opens the trunk and counts out five grand from the giant stash of money in a canvas duffel bag, gives it to Jones.

"I take it that's not even yours." Jones nods at the money.

"Now you understand my urgency."

Jones folds the money and stuffs it in his back pocket. "Don't call me again." Then walks away.

"Thanks for the ride, Jonesie," Conner yells after him. Jones says nothing, just gets in his car and drives off.

Also in the trunk is a roll of duct tape. Conner grabs it, rips a lengthy piece off and quickly wraps it around his wife's head, covering her mouth as she struggles against him. He slaps her, and she falls against the car, crying.

"You didn't even know that kid, did you? Fuckin' slut." Conner opens the passenger door and shoves his wife in. He grabs the tape and binds her hands and feet, then he hops in the driver's seat, adjusts the rearview mirror after she'd knocked it around during the struggle. "I can't believe you'd do me like that. I treated you good, Diane. I bought you jewelry, took you out. Shit, I bought you a fuckin' car. You ever had a man who's done that?"

Diane whines through the tape, and her body writhes like a maggot against the door. Snot bubbles from her nose, eyes burning red with tears.

Conner sees Shasta running toward the car. It's time to go. He starts the car, and Shasta gets in the backseat. "He's all fucked up," Shasta says.

"Is he dead?" Conner asks.

"I fucked him up real good."

"But is he dead!?"

"You hit him with the gun three fuckin' times before I even got to him, Connie. He was probably gone before you left the room."

Diane shuts her eyes tight, wincing, and soaks the front of her dress with more tears.

CHAPTER 22: SHASTA, CONNER, AND DIANE

Along the dark desert road, the tires seem louder than normal. They drive for twenty minutes without a word between them, only the quiet whimpering of Diane as she sits against the door, her head on the window.

In the rearview, Conner catches Shasta run a finger under his nose, closing his eyes in what seems to be a moment of perverted ecstasy. Conner digs his nails into the steering wheel, then slows the car and pulls over.

"I gotta piss," he says. "Come on, Shasta. We gotta figure something out, you and me."

Shasta gets out of the car, takes one last hit from a cigarette and flicks it into the black sky. It hits dirt, and sparks fly—a firework show for the ants.

The two walk a distance from the car,

farther than they need to for just a piss and a chat.

Conner says, "What are we gonna do, Shasta?"

"Good question. I've been thinkin'—"

"I mean about you." Conner pulls the gun from his waistband and points it at his friend.

Shasta throws his arms in the air, and his eyes bulge with fear. "Woah, man. Connie…what's this?"

Again, Conner thinks of Jones and Rochester and that girl's knees. "A few years ago, there was this guy, used to work with me. We did runs together. He'd take a little off the top here and there. And more than once, when we were making a run, we'd be at a store, and the guy would pocket candy bars, or a tallboy from the cooler. He'd steal 'em. He even took a whole fifth from the shelf once, stuck it in his coat and walked out. It's like he couldn't help himself. He had what's called…sticky fingers."

"I didn't steal nothing from you, Connie. I swear. I been nothing but loyal. You know me…I'd never do nothin' like that." Shasta pushes the hat off his forehead and lets the sweat bead.

"You know how else you get sticky fingers, Shasta?"

Conner watches his friend's face intently, waiting for a sign that says the words have finally clicked. But either Shasta is dumber than Conner thought, or he's got one hell of a poker face, because the same stone-faced fear is stuck there.

"Let me smell your finger, Shasta."

And there's the epiphany.

"You've got at least one there that smells like ass…or pussy. My wife's pussy."

"Connie, I—"

The gun goes off, and Shasta's head falls back. The cowboy hat drops, and the oily sprigs of hair stay matted to his head until his body hits the dirt, where they bounce and land again.

CHAPTER 23: DIANE AND CONNER

Diane watches them walk and sees Conner pull the gun, but she doesn't expect him to pull the trigger. This is not the Conner she thought she knew. While hindsight gives her a better idea of who he really was when they met, killing old friends is not part of the equation she's been putting together.

Even if Conner saw what Shasta had done to her in the hotel room, it's still not enough. There must be a history here she's not aware of, and the assault merely the catalyst for ending it all.

While she never did like Shasta—and even less after the groping—a bullet to the head is not something she would have wished for. A good ass whipping? Fuck yes. Maybe even a hand full of broken fingers. But murder? Definitely not.

This side of Conner, whether it be something new, or just undiscovered by her, she needs to tame it. Four months of marriage is not enough to stop a bullet.

As Conner walks back to the car, she thinks of her next move. *I'll thank him for killing Shasta, make him think we're on the same page, that I recognize the heroic redemption displayed.*

Conner gets back in the car and reaches for the glovebox, pulls out a handkerchief and wipes the gun down thoroughly, then hands it to Diane. "Hold this a minute."

She thinks he's joking but takes it, her wrists joined together by duct tape. And without another thought, she quickly aims the gun at his chest and pulls the trigger. A click. But no boom.

He grins. "Perfect." And with his hand wrapped in the handkerchief, he takes the gun from her. "Now if you try leaving, or fucking with me in any way, the blood is on your hands. Shasta killed your boy toy, and you killed Shasta. The pervert even has a little of your DNA for safekeeping. Open and shut case, as they say."

Diane groans under the tape and slams her head against the window.

"You don't fuck with Conner Sibbald, baby."

CHAPTER 24: CAKE
One Week Later

Cake opens his eyes, sees a tiled ceiling, hears beeps, smells bleached linen. He moves his eyes, the only thing that doesn't hurt. A strange man sits in a chair six feet away.

"Nurse!" the man says, then quickly leaves.

It only takes a moment for Cake to realize he's in a hospital. It takes longer to realize why. He remembers making love to Diane, spending the night in paradise with an angel. The courtyard, the amber lights, the food and wine. Periwinkle toes. But that's all. He sits up, and the room spins. An IV juts from his arm.

A nurse comes into the room, followed by the strange man. He's scruffy with an unkempt beard, dirty jeans, and a baseball cap with graying hair that pours out in curls.

The man is quiet, watching the nurse as she checks Cake's eyes, pulling at his lids and shining the brightest light he's ever seen into them.

"How are you feeling, Mr. Donaldson?" the nurse asks.

"Tired…confused."

"Do you remember your name?"

"Cake."

"And do you recognize this man?"

Cake looks at the man again, who anxiously awaits a reply, a look of worry across his face.

"No."

"It's me, Cake. Your dad."

Cake squints, imagines the beard gone, the hair shorter. Finally, the bulbous, rosacea-covered nose gives him away. It is his dad. "Why?"

"They called me last week. I've been here ever since, son. Right here by your side."

Waking up in the hospital makes no sense, his father spending time with him makes even less.

"You were in a coma."

The nurse turns to the aging man and

in an almost whispering tone, says, "Sir, I'm going to get Dr. Campisi, and then we'll reveal what's happened and where to go from here, okay? In the meantime, try and keep the conversation simple."

The nurse leaves, and Cake's father pulls a chair close to the bed, sits down. "I know I haven't been around much."

Cake feels the bandage on his head, the bandage on his nose, and runs his tongue over his teeth, making sure they're all there. "That's an understatement."

"I was young, Cake. I didn't know what—"

"You didn't know what you were doing...I know. We've had this conversation before, Jerry. Many times."

His father sighs, sits back in the chair. "You don't have to call me Dad. I get it, but it's nice to know I'm still your go-to when shit hits the fan."

"How are you my go-to?"

"You wrote me down at the diner as your emergency contact." Jerry smiles.

"Had to put something."

"It ain't much, but I'll take it.

"We in Glover?"

"Yep. In Glover General. Right where you were born. I was there that day, son." Jerry smiles, and the leather in his face cracks. "The hell happened, anyway?"

"Do you know a guy named Conner? Some kind of mob guy, sorta."

"The mob?" Jerry scootches the chair closer to the bed, lowers his voice. "Son… you in some kinda trouble?"

"I was."

"What's Conner's last name?"

Cake panics when he realizes he has no idea Diane's full name, which means no way of checking on her, making sure she's okay.

"I don't even know. Drives a Thunderbird, wears a suit, dark hair…Hell, I don't know shit about him." Cake winces at the pain in his head.

"They said you was in New Mexico… lying on a hotel room floor. I looked up the hotel, Cake. Where'd you get that kinda money?"

"It wasn't mine…I was staying with a friend. Listen, I appreciate the visit, but can we end this? I got nothing to say to you, and I still can't figure out why you're here except maybe thinking I've got my hands on money now and you want a piece of it."

"Lord, son. It ain't like that. I'm here cuz you're my boy."

"I've been your boy for twenty-two years now. You're just now figuring that out?"

"I guess getting that call, finding out you might die, it puts things into perspective."

"And you didn't want to live the rest of your life feeling guilty, so you thought you'd make things right, make sure it's off your conscience."

"You're right...you *don't* know shit, boy."

"And there he is...that's the Jerry Donaldson I know."

"Fuck this." Jerry shoves the chair behind him, and it crashes against the wall. "I try and make amends, and you gotta go and be an asshole about it."

"Yep...I'm the asshole. By the way, thanks for keeping it simple. Nothing like waking from a coma and going straight into whatever the hell it is you're looking for."

"Ya know...you'd think with your mom dead you'd be a little more appreciative of someone who's trying to give a shit."

"Jerry..." Cake stews, conjuring words to put the man in his place but at the last minute thinks better of it. "Just get out. You can die happy now. You said your peace."

"Yes, I did. I tried my damnedest. It's you who needs to change." Jerry points a nicotine-stained finger. "Not me."

"Bye, Jerry."

"Ungrateful bastard." His father storms out and tries to slam the door but the rubber stopper kills the effort, and the man grunts as his arm is nearly pulled from its socket. "Fuckin' prick cursing everything you touch."

If Cake weren't so used to it, he'd cry about now, but he just rolls his eyes and almost finds comfort in his father's harsh exit. Forgiving and forgetting is not something he has the mental stamina to do right now, particularly when it's clear his old man hasn't changed a bit.

The doctor comes in and explains to Cake he's been in a coma for seven days, suffered a brain injury, an orbital fracture, six broken ribs, and a broken nose that's been set. According to the doctor, the nose should be "good as new" once it heals. He asks Cake what he remembers. Cake lies and tells a story about some random thugs in the hotel mugging him but never got a look at them, not even so much as a silhouette.

"Any cops been in here to ask questions?" Cake says.

"No, they haven't. After a day or two, you can reach out to them and file a report. But for now, I think it's best you give your mind a rest."

Whether it be from fear of Conner and his people, or he just doesn't want the hassle, Cake decides to let it die. But as far as finding Diane, that's something he's not willing to let go of.

CHAPTER 25: CAKE

Cake spends three more days in the hospital for observation. As far as brain damage, he's given a good bill of health, with strict instructions from the doctor not to lift or exercise for at least the next four to six weeks and to come back in if he develops headache, blurry vision, or memory loss.

He dips into his savings and decides moving is a good idea. Lucille had visited him in the hospital and filled him in on what Conner put her through. She felt bad about giving up his locale so offered the name of her cousin who owns some real estate. "Some of it's run down," she'd said. "But he's a good landlord. Something goes wrong in your place, and he's on top of it."

Cake decides to use the lead and gets a small, two-bedroom house through her cousin. The rent isn't much because you can't drink the tap water, and the thermostat doesn't go past sixty-eight. But the interior itself is remodeled with fresh paint, carpeting, and new outlets, as well as windows. From the outside, he's seen better walls on tree forts. But from the inside, he'd expect to pay at least double what he does.

He moves fast, within forty-eight hours. He mostly follows doctor's orders and lifts nothing heavy, instead pays a few neighborhood kids to haul his furniture, bed, and CDs. Because he breaks the lease on his old place, he eats the deposit.

He applies for a job at four restaurants, two factories, and an automotive garage. Cake doesn't know as much about cars as he does cooking an egg over easy, but it's an apprentice position specifically for novice mechanics. Two days later, they call him. Forty-five hours a week, paying two dollars more than what he was making at the diner.

In less than a week after leaving the hospital, Cake Donaldson has a brand-new life, yet the thought of Diane and what has become of her keeps the joy at bay. After hearing Lucille's report of what Conner did, he expects the man to be in prison.

Apparently, he's got more pull than Cake thought. This might explain why the cops never reached out.

Cake sits on his couch, a beer in hand, the TV on but turned down. His body hurts, his face still swollen. The house feels empty. He hates the idea of Diane thinking she was so close to freedom, then pulled back into the cage.

If she's even alive.

He spends the next hour googling Conner's name and associating it with Glover, along with other keywords like "Mr. and Mrs. Conner" and "Conner and Diane", using the names in various cities just outside Glover. Nothing helpful comes up. He vaguely recalls Diane giving Conner's last name when mocking him. *"He'll use me as an example of what happens when you cross Conner...Something."* It starts with a B or an L. Maybe an S or a C.

He searches for a report of the incident at the diner and finds the article reported by The Glover Gazette but no mention of suspects, only the words "still at large." Not even a description of either car, which he knows damn well everyone saw.

Fuck it. He calls the police.

"Yeah, I'm calling to report some information regarding the hostage situation at Skipp's Diner a few weeks ago."

He's asked to hold. It feels like a waste of time. If the police weren't paid off, they'd have gotten with him by now. This is going nowhere.

"This is Lieutenant Shay."

Cake gives the officer his name and tells him he was there, that he's the one who was in the coma at Glover General. He tells him everything, every detail he can remember. Conner hitting the john, meeting Diane, them leaving, and the money in the trunk. He changes the story slightly, making it seem like Diane discovered the money after the fact.

The lieutenant listens, never asks a single question. Cake is right. Waste of time.

"Thank you for the information, Mr. Donaldson. We'll call you if we need anything else. In the meantime, I'd advise you to keep this information to yourself, just to be on the safe side."

Waste of fucking time.

CHAPTER 26: CAKE

His first day at work, he drops Conner's name to a coworker but gives no other details. The guy says he doesn't know a single person by that name. Cake decides it's too dangerous asking questions around people he doesn't know. And if they did know Conner, they'd never say.

Diane had made it sound like the people he works for are a disorganized mess. A joke. But so far, Conner is untouchable.

For the next four weeks, Cake's ribs heal, and his face loses the yellow-purple hue. He works hard, grabbing extra hours when he can and drops the search for Conner and Diane, except for the occasional Google search. Still nothing.

A few paychecks come and go, and he dips into what little savings he has left, remodels the extra bedroom, spending hundreds on decor and supplies he hopes will one day come to use. He's proud of the room.

One day, he shows up for work and the Thunderbird is there. Two bullet holes and a broken window that needs repairing. Cake's stomach seizes with a fist full of nails.

"What's the story here?" he asks Randy. Randy is the senior mechanic at Glover Fine Auto who's been mentoring him. He almost trusts the guy, but not enough to let on he knows who owns the car and why it's in the shape it is.

"Needs a new panel, new trunk, and window."

"I mean this." Cake points to the perfectly round hole in the trunk. "That a bullet hole?"

"Looks like it. Probably a drive-by. I've learned not to ask, ya know? We're just here to do a job."

The urge to ask about the car's owner is tempting. But he can't. If Randy is somehow associated with Conner, it'll mean more than just losing his job. Much more.

"Yeah, good thinking," is all he says.

He can find out more through one of two ways, stalk the office and wait for an opportunity to access the computer, miraculously stumbling across an electronic record of the transaction with Conner. Or he can wait until the job is done, when they call the client for pickup, something they've had Cake do before.

Judging by what he's learned and how fast the garage works, he's got at least two days before the car is ready. By then, if all he gets is Conner's full name, it should be enough to track down his address.

CHAPTER 27: DIANE

She sits by the pool, an old paperback in hand. She's not sunbathing because she hates it now when Conner gets any glimpse of her body. She tries to forget who she's married to and lives a lie, doing her best to enjoy the spoils. Good food, a nice house with all the furnishings, expensive clothes, and a flatscreen that covers half the wall, which she escapes with day after day using a plethora of brainless programming. Her only hope is one day Conner will tire of her. Tire of the same piece of ass, the unenthusiastic sex, and he'll be the one to leave, finally setting her free.

As she reads, the words don't register. She thinks of Cake, harboring guilt for dragging him into Conner's world of crime, which up until that night she perceived as tamer than it is. With a stumbling team like Shasta and Conner and all his insecurities, it never felt this threatening.

But now, the term mob actually feels appropriate. She has witnessed the paying off of law enforcement and politicians, the mysterious guests who show up at the house for their sit-downs, and the small bits of conversation she overhears. The threat of being framed isn't what keeps her trapped, it's Conner erasing her very existence, tossing her in a barrel, burned and buried in the desert. She knows he has it in him.

Weeks ago, she considered mocking Stockholm syndrome, convincing Conner that despite everything he's done, she loves him and is happy. But that's movie bullshit, and Conner is smarter than that. Instead, she plays the dull housewife. The kind where the husband eventually looks outside the marriage for his needs. Then communication dies, the sex nonexistent, and the marriage dissolves. A much better plan.

She holds little hope Cake is still alive, though reminds herself that other than his assault on her, Shasta didn't seem to have the cold heart Conner does. She has a hard time picturing the greasy man killing someone, although the same could have been said about her husband, until he murdered his own friend that dark, chaotic night.

"How about a home-cooked meal for a change?" Conner's voice behind her. He's standing in the threshold of the slider in his shorts and no shirt. The sight of him disgusts her.

"Okay." She agrees, only because boxed macaroni and cheese is what's on the menu, perhaps a salad on the side just to make it look convincing, that yes, she really is that dumb. That dull. And he should get himself a new girl.

"I'll be home around six. Open a bottle of wine while you're at it."

"Got it." *Mac and cheese with wine. We can drink it with straws.* She flips the page in her book with a smile he can't see.

She hears the door shut, the car start, and puts the book down, which feels more like a screen to hide her disgust and contempt.

The first two weeks after that night in Santa Fe, she scoured the local paper, looking for mention of Cake—a police report, an obituary. Shasta didn't have time to dispose of a body. Could Conner have had someone else deal with it? Maybe the big guy in the hallway. Was he Conner's "cleaner?"

She finds it tragic that just a few details stop her from finding out more. Cake's last name, his address. A friend's name, a parent, a favorite place in town he loved to spend time at, like in the movies where the lover knows just where to find them at the perfect time—at that park where the ducks float on a pond made of glass, a hiking path that leads to a breathtaking scenery, or the grave of a loved one.

She knows of Marianne, who had left for school four years ago, breaking Cake's heart. And then there's the diner. But no way in hell is she going back there. She'll be the witch they burn at the stake. Or worse yet, Conner will find out. He'll know what she's up to. And if Cake isn't dead already, he will be. And so will she.

Asking Conner outright if Cake is dead, that's off the table. Him catching her in bed with the man is a wound that needs to stay closed. It took nearly three weeks for him to stop mentioning daily what she'd done, reminding her what it feels like for a husband to see his wife sprawled naked next to another man. Hearing the word husband has become a foreign thing that doesn't belong. He isn't a husband. He's a warden.

She heads inside, rummages through Conner's dresser drawers. She's done it many times in the past month but hasn't found a single clue. She's never even sure what she's looking for. Finding a postcard with Cake's full name and address is about as likely as Conner making amends to her one-night lover by inviting him over for a ménage á trois. But she looks anyway, any chance she gets. The only thing she ever finds is a package of condoms. They give her hope that Conner is moving on, trapping some other woman in his web. But the condoms are still unopened and have been for weeks.

She's never even run across the gun he threatened to frame her with. Not that it would help, but it tells her there is a place where secrets are kept, though she suspects that place is not in their house. Conner would never leave her alone to find it.

Frustrated, she throws herself on the couch and cries. The cushions have seen an ocean of tears over the past several weeks, taken wild punches, absorbed a hundred screams, and ignored a thousand prayers.

CHAPTER 28: CAKE

Two days have passed, and Cake is helping install a new window in the Thunderbird. It's the last repair needed before the call is made. Who makes the calls is completely random. Randy could walk right into the office and do it without saying a word. He could ask Sam, the other mechanic. Or find himself too busy and ask Cake to handle it, which is how it's been the past few weeks.

The window is installed, the door panel secured in position, and the window washed with cleaner. Randy lights a cigarette and steps just outside the garage, shields his eyes from the sun and spits on the ground. Cake is glued to his every move, watching for a tell that now is the time. Finally, he can't wait for the desired request and desperately belts out, "Hey, Randy. You want me to call this guy?" throwing his thumb toward the Thunderbird.

"Sure. Have Sam get you the name and…actually." The mechanic reaches into his pocket and pulls out a small wad of cash. "Can you run across the street and grab some burritos. Get whatever you want. It's on me. Sam likes the bean with extra sour cream. I'll take beef. No sour cream, extra guac." He offers the money to Cake, who's stomach goes sour, his throat dry.

"Yeah, okay." He walks up to Randy and takes the twenty being offered. "I'll make the call when I get back."

Randy excuses the idea with a wave of his hand. "Don't even worry about it. I'll get it. Oh…and grab a bunch of that green sauce. A ton of it. I put that shit on everything. It's like my ketchup." He laughs, and the sound feels like a last chance at happiness stomped into gravel.

Cake struggles to hide his disappointment, which looks more like white-knuckled panic, then sprints across the street, hoping the line is short, the cook is fast, and Randy gets sidetracked.

He throws open the door of Nina's Taqueria, and a collection of bells ring above. Two people are ahead of him in line. They're together, ordering what feels like one of everything on the menu.

Cake can see Randy from here. He's still smoking his cigarette, staring at the sky, and shielding his eyes, as though daring the sun to burn him blind.

Nearly five minutes go by. It's a lifetime in hell. Finally, no one stands between him and the counter. He frantically recites the order. He says it too fast, and the girl at the counter asks him to repeat it. He does, with eyes on Randy who has given up his fight with the sun and is flicking his smoke into the afternoon breeze. As Randy walks toward the office, Cake looks away. He can't watch anymore. His stomach swirls with bile that kicks and claws, threatening to tear a hole in him.

Cake pays for the order and pockets the change. He can see the cook in the back, moving his arms like they're underwater, punching through molasses, taking too much time, too much pride in his work.

If he misses getting Conner's info, he'll tail him when he comes to get the Bird, leaving work if he has to. Even if it means losing his job. Another job can be had, but this is his last chance of ever finding out if Diane is okay, finding out if he can help her escape again. Escape for good.

A highlight reel from that night in the hotel flashes on the screen in his head. The way they made love, like two high-school lovers discovering each other's bodies for the first time on prom night, away from their looming parents. The thrill of getting caught, dangerously taboo.

The girl at the counter wakes him from his trance as she pushes a bag of food toward him. "Here you are, sir. Have a good day."

Somehow, he remembers the green sauce and sees a wooden bin filled with it. He grabs as many as one fist can carry and crams them into the bag, then turns and runs for the door.

Traffic stops his beeline, and he's forced to wait. He can see Randy standing in the doorway of the office, telephone to his ear. It's too late. He's making the call. Cake loses the urgency in his step as he walks across the street once the traffic clears.

He stands next to Randy, bag of food in hand, and looks at the computer screen, hoping Conner's info will still be there. The screen is black.

"Yeah, we can do all that," Randy says into the phone. "What we'll do is run diagnostics on the car so we can pinpoint what's going on…Sure, bring it on down anytime. We close at six…You betcha. Have a good day, now." Randy hangs the phone up. It didn't sound like he was talking to Conner but an inquiring customer.

"Here you go, Randy," Cake says. "Beef, no sour cream, extra guacamole."

"Great…let's eat. Sam! Food's here."

Sam peeks his head out from around the corner. "Be right there."

Cake says to Randy, "I think I'll hold off on mine for a bit. In the meantime, I can make that call if you like." He prays it hasn't already been done.

"Yeah…sure, man. Let me pull him up." Randy enters the office and moves the mouse. The screen goes from black to a half-naked blonde on the beach, covered in sand and beads of water. He fiddles with the keyboard, and up pops the number of Conner Sibbald as well as an address Cake puts to memory—189 Woodale Drive. "There it is. Tell him we're all set. Right here's the total." Randy points to a receipt he's already filled out, listing the work done, as well as the make and model of the car.

Randy opens the bag of food, rummages through the three burritos until he finds his, then snatches four of the packets of green sauce, and leaves the office, making way for Cake in the tiny room.

Cake heads in, grabs the phone off the wall, and dials the number. As he listens for the first ring, paranoia hits like a steamroller. What if Conner can tell it's him? Even though he's never heard his voice.

On the third ring, a female voice says hello. Cake's heart gallops, his skin goes cold. He's both terrified and elated. He didn't anticipate Diane picking up.

He fumbles over the first few words, while introducing himself as calling from Glover Fine Auto on Worthington. "Uhh... I'm looking for Conner Sibbald."

The voice on the other end hesitates, then says, "He's not here."

Cake wants to tell her it's him, that he's been looking for her and it's so good to hear her voice, knowing she's okay. But if Conner is actually home and just doesn't want to be bothered, she'll never be able to hide the shock at Cake's announcement. Shit would go south real fast over at 189 Woodale Drive. "Okay, could you just tell him his car is ready?"

Diane seems to hesitate again, then, "Cake?"

"Diane! Yes…yes, it's me."

"Oh God, Cake. You're alive."

"Are you okay? I mean…you're still with him, I guess. But you're okay?"

"Oh, Cake. I'm only here because I don't have a choice. I've been so worried about you. I thought for sure you were dead. Shasta said…It doesn't matter. It's so good to hear your voice. I can't believe you're calling."

"Believe it or not, I'm calling because Conner's car is ready." He chuckles.

"You're a mechanic?"

"For now, yeah."

"Not a singer in a cowboy hat?" Cake can hear the smile behind her words.

"I don't even know what to say. I've tried finding you but had nothing to go by. I don't even know your full name."

"Sibbald. My name is Diane Marie Sibbald, but my maiden name is Sparrows. My birthday is December twenty-eighth, nineteen-eighty-nine. Don't let me go missing again." This time he hears the pain in her voice.

"I won't, Ms. Sparrows." Cake turns his head so Randy and Sam don't see the toothy smile. "I need to see you."

"Shit, Cake…How? Conner is more connected than I thought. I can't trust anyone anymore. I don't know who he knows and who he doesn't."

"I want to show you something. I got a new place, and—"

"Oh, sweetie. I just don't know."

Cake hates himself for even asking. It's far too dangerous, and what they had is gone. It was a short journey he'll never forget. Be thankful for the memories and the moment. She's alive. So are you. Be grateful.

But is she truly alive?

"Diane…Are you a prisoner there?"

She doesn't say anything. And he can't tell if it's her way of answering with the obvious or because she's choking on tears.

"You can't live like this," he says.

"I know." Her voice cracks.

"You need to get out of there. But this time, no money. Don't give Conner a reason to bring some posse after us." He looks over at Randy and Sam. They're busy with their lunch—overly stuffed tortillas in their fists, mashing them into their faces.

Diane is silent again, as though quietly encouraging Cake to talk her into it.

"We'll leave the country and head to Mexico," he adds.

"We barely know each other, Cake. And when you're in your forties, I'll be—"

"You'll be in your fifties. Stop with the age thing. I'm not in high school. And you're right. We barely know each other, but that doesn't mean it can't work. I'm no asshole, and neither are you. That should be enough."

"But you want to wear a cowboy hat and boots. I hate that shit." She laughs through a cry.

"Maybe you'll learn to love it, and you can get your own."

The phone falls silent, as though they're both considering pulling the trigger. Or just ending it now. Finally, "Give me your address," she says. "And meet me there tomorrow at ten thirty p.m."

"Pack my bags?" he says.

A long and scared sigh. "Yes."

Cake gives her his address and phone number in case anything comes up before then. "We can do this, Diane. We can set you free."

"I believe you, hon. It's fucking crazy, but I believe you."

CHAPTER 29: CAKE

Cake packs nothing but clothes, a few CDs, and a toothbrush. Everything else can stay behind. He started over once. He can do it again.

He makes sure there's nothing in the house that may hint at their destination. No travel brochures, laptop full of google searches on Mexican hotels, or MapQuest directions. But there isn't. Everything was done on his phone, secure in his pants pocket.

He wonders if he could have done this had his mother still been alive, just up and leave, kicking Glover dirt off his heels. Probably not. This kind of spontaneity is for those with no family, no heart stretched across friends. This is for those who have nothing but what the next day holds.

He spends the rest of the day filling the trunk with other necessities just in case. Gas station food, water, Winstons, blankets, and a baseball bat. He gets an oil change, has the fluids checked, tire pressure, making sure the car is up for the task of making an eight-hour drive to the border.

Sitting back on a bed he'll never sleep in again, he thinks of writing a note to the landlord, or at least to Lucille. But with a man like Conner on the hunt, it's best to make this an unexpected disappearing act. No paper trail. No clues. Not a soul on the planet knows a thing.

Cell phones! Those three days he spent in the hospital after waking from the coma offered countless hours of reflection, and it was there he realized her phone was their downfall. Conner couldn't have trailed them stealthily from the road. It was her phone. He'd been tracking her, most likely from the very day they met, making sure he knew where his woman was at all times. Fucking cell phones. A drug for the lazy, entertainment for the bored, a trap for the possessive.

He wants to call Diane, let her know to leave the cell at home, smash the fucker against the wall and burn the card. But he can't chance it. Not this close to her freedom. They'll ditch it before they leave Glover, along with his. Then they'll grab a map. Kick it old school.

Cake gets up, walks over to the extra bedroom he'd remodeled, stands in the doorway and smiles. The room is a passion project. Not his passion, someone else's. It was never for him.

He looks at the clock on the living room wall—the only thing hanging. Ten o'clock. The minutes slide by like sap on a cold, winter day.

CHAPTER 30: CONNER

He drives the newly repaired Thunderbird behind a plaza, parks next to the rear entrance to Liberty Liquor Store. Coswell's inside, so is Bennie. They're talking about a deal that's going down tomorrow night. Drugs are involved, which is something Conner never wanted to be a part of. Not because of some moral code but the risk. Eventually, he caved. Afterall, it's just hash.

Coswell is Conner's boss. He's the big man before the bigger man. The bigger man doesn't live in Texas but Southern California, with the rest of The Candlemen.

Bennie is a sidekick and looks like one. Short, fat, with a face that melted into a thick frown before he hit thirty. Fish lips. He's never seen without a vest over a white button-down, the vest always too small, the pits of the shirt pus colored.

Conner has a key to the door and uses

it, walks in. Locks the door. He can hear the murmur of voices down the hall, the screech of chair legs, the smell of hot coffee and cigars. He walks down the hall and into a large room with a table in the center. Cliché.

"Speak of the devil," Coswell says, and Conner hopes nothing but good was being said.

"Get the car fixed?" Bennie asks.

"Good as new."

"I told ya. They're the best in town. And no questions asked."

"You guys start without me or you just havin' a circle jerk?" Conner pulls a chair up. The legs sound like a woman dying. It echoes in the large room.

"Started as a jerk," Coswell says. "But Bennie couldn't find his pecker." The three cough laughter until Coswell slaps a hand on the table between them to change the subject and the tone. "Alright then…change of plans. Just a slight one. The big man has to be in Afghan day after tomorrow, so this shipment we have, it's gotta be picked up tonight. Midnight sharp." Coswell looks at the other two, studies them. "Now, I ain't happy about it either, but the good news is, because of this minor inconvenience, there's a little something extra for everyone, which I've been granted permission to give you early." He slides an envelope to Bennie and one to Conner. They both open them and flip through the bills inside.

"I can deal with that," Conner says.

"Most definitely." Bennie slaps his stack against the palm of his hand and sticks it inside his too-tight vest.

"Connie, that means you'll have to take the Thunderbird home and swap it. I don't want that car around any of these deals. Not since what happened with your wife. Brings too much attention."

"You got it."

"I know we planned on a pow-wow with an evening of cards, but we best get started on the drive. In your envelopes are the directions. We're driving separately, but I'll be there. We'll meet at the first spot marked on the map I gave you, then we'll head in together." Coswell slams his hand on the table again to signify meeting adjourned. "Sound good?"

"See ya soon."

Chair legs scream, and the men head down the hall and out the door. Conner gets in the Thunderbird and heads home, where he's not expected for several hours.

CHAPTER 31: CONNER

With a little time to kill, Conner stops at the store for a bottle of wine. He and Diane polished off the last the other night. He drank most of it and noticed she barely touched it. The bitch had been like that all month, but she'll figure it out. She'll realize how well she has it. Bills paid, a nice house, nice clothes, doesn't have to work. There's a million women out there that'd kill for what she has.

He grabs the most expensive bottle he can find, sets it on the counter, and asks for a pack of Winstons for the ungrateful whore. He looks through the Bic lighters that sit in a rack on the counter. Tie-dye, marijuana leaves, polka-dots, and even one with a large-mouth bass jumping out of water. He grabs a simple white Bic and sets it on the counter next to the wine, pays the clerk, and heads out.

When he gets in the car, he notices

a gum wrapper on the passenger seat floorboard. He knows it's from Diane, and it triggers a thought. She let that asshole drive his baby. He wonders if they fucked in the car and how many times and which seats. By the time he pulls onto his street, he's worked himself up, But the questions he has disappear when a new one arises, one that's far more important.

What the fuck is Diane doing pulling out of the driveway in his other car?

CHAPTER 32: CAKE

It's 10:37. Diane still hasn't shown. He doesn't dare call. Not yet. Maybe she got hung up in traffic, forgot her suitcase, got lost. She'll be here.

Cake sits on the couch, scratching designs into its suede arm, erases them away, draws more. His foot taps to a song in his head he doesn't know the name of, only the chorus, which he recalls has nothing to do with the actual title.

He hears a car approaching, runs to the window. A pickup truck drives by. He paces between the front door and into the kitchen, then back again. When he's in the kitchen for the eighth time, he grabs a glass of water, then sees headlights paint the walls. Someone's in the driveway.

He runs to the window by the front door, looks out but doesn't recognize the car. It's not the Thunderbird. Thank God. If it is Diane, he doesn't want her bringing that thing here. He hates the sight of it. While there were some good memories in the seats—discussions that hurt, discussions that healed and provoked thought, ones that tore down walls—the thing is really Conner's yellow swinging dick he hopes he'll never see again.

Outside, the driver's side door of the car opens, and the dome light springs to life. It's Diane. Butterflies in the stomach are cute. These are piranha, chipping away. It's a familiar feeling. Fear, excitement, and maybe love wrapped in a bouncing ball filled with teeth.

He puts his hand on the doorknob and opens it, as her sandals hit the walk. Her smile lights the darkened street, and her stride picks up, then turns to a run as she drops her suitcase and rushes toward Cake.

His arms are open, inviting. When their bodies hit, it's the perfect breathy storm of passion. A Hollywood kiss. Lips parting, tongues dancing, tears falling. Life has never felt so worth living.

She pushes him through the door, hands traveling, almost violently. He wants to rip her clothes off. She wants them ripped off. But they need to leave. He pulls away as she bites his lip. "Your phone. We have to get rid of it." He heads back in for more.

"What do you mean?" Every word is spoken through curled lips and heavy breath.

"That's how he found us before. He's tracking you."

"Shit..." She pulls away, dips her hands into the back pocket of her jeans that fit like skin. "What do I do with it?"

Cake grabs the phone, drops it on the floor, and stomps on it until more than just the screen is cracked. He spots the sim card among the bits, snatches it, runs to the bathroom, and flushes the tiny card down the toilet.

Diane follows him, but her attention is directed elsewhere. She's staring at the extra bedroom, where Cake has spent so much money, so much time and effort. Giant blank canvases cover the walls, a large table runs along them, filled with various paints in a vast rainbow of colors—acrylics, oils, watercolor. There are brushes, palettes, pads of paper, clean rags, gouache.

A large easel sits in one corner holding a blank canvas, while another smaller easel sits on yet another table. And in the center of it all is an adjustable drafting table with a comfortable office chair made of leather.

Diane's eyes bulge with tears as she enters the room, Cake following behind. The tears can hold no longer and fall to the floor of the art studio built for her. "You did this…for me?"

Cake just smiles, maybe bigger than he ever has.

"I…I don't even know what to say."

"Sometimes a moment births the perfect words. Right?"

Her face gleefully contorts, and she nods while more tears flow. Her head tilts to the side as the two lock eyes. The way she looks deep into him, the lines around her mouth deepening from painful elation. He takes a mental snapshot to remember always, her first day of freedom. He's not a man with expectations, with a forceful hand and poison tongue. She no longer has to provide or pretend. She's free with him.

Before either of them can react to the shouted words of "You stupid fuckin' whore!" behind them, Diane's hair spreads like petals as her head snaps forward, and every canvas in the room is showered with crimson.

CHAPTER 33: CAKE, DIANE, AND CONNER

Instinct causes Cake to cower, shielding his face with his arm. After an explosion of sound, he feels the pelting of blood but isn't sure what it is. Another explosion, and a hole rips through the loose armpit of his shirt.

In one brief moment that seems slow enough for comprehension that Conner is there and firing a gun, Cake springs forward. Another explosion burns a hole in his thigh, but his momentum keeps him on target. He lands on Conner, sending them both to the ground.

Cake grabs the man's wrists, slamming them into the hardwood floor. This is the first time he's really seen Conner Sibbald's face, the rage in his eyes, the gritting teeth. This is the face his lover has had to answer to, be fearful of. Somewhere under this devil's skin is a mask well worn —a trap that lured a beautiful woman until she forgot who she was.

The gun goes off again, but the bullet soars toward the ceiling. Conner rips a hand free, and Cake manages to swing a fist at the devil's nose. Not a hook, but a jackhammer. The sound of snapping twigs brings a geyser of blood. Cake drills him again and feels a tooth give under the driven weight of a knuckle.

Conner's grip on the gun loosens, and Cake grabs it. No time is given to think, other than the quick biting reality that happiness lay crumpled in a bloody heap behind him.

With the barrel of the gun jammed into the jealous man's chest, Cake pulls the trigger twice, sending Conner Sibbald to the grave.

Cake barely feels the pain in his leg. It's his stomach that carries it, the crushing of his heart. With a grieving moan, he pushes himself off the dead man's body and crawls to the woman he wanted so badly to see freed from another's oppressive grip.

She's face down, her hair almost covering the hole in the back of her head. He doesn't dare turn her over. The snapshot he took just moments before will have to last a lifetime. The picture plays in his head for one quick moment, then burns away like the melting of celluloid on a projector screen, as he imagines the blank and lifeless stare that now resides where the smile once sat. And of the trio of smiles that began this whole short journey toward finding love again.

He puts a trembling arm around her, buries his face into her back, and for the first time in years, cries.

CHAPTER 34: CAKE

One Week Later

Cake Donaldson walks out of Glover General for the second time this summer but with a limp in his gait. This time, the police did come talk to him. Not the locals. These were state officers. He faces no charges, and the officers subtly alluded to him being a hero, that Conner Sibbald had been a scourge for far too long, and with him gone they're hoping the investigation will lead to others, as they ransack every bit of real estate he owns.

Cake has no idea if there are others within Conner's circle he needs to worry about. He doubts it, since he's now in the spotlight, and it sounds like Conner's buddies are on the verge of bars and need to lay low. But if there is a price on his head, looking over his shoulder is a habit he refuses to start. Losing the prospect of love tends to offer a nice helping of *Don't Give a*

Fuck.

He takes a cab home and stands in front of his house, stares at the front door, considers what's on the other side. The bullet holes, Diane's shattered phone. The canvases that are no longer blank.

He looks at the car. The trunk is still full. Clothing, music, food. It's an easy choice. He hops in and backs out, heads down the street with no destination, except one quick stop before the new chapter begins—down on Worthington to pick up one of them cowboy hats. And maybe a pair of boots.

To subscribe to my newsletter, visit www.chadlutzke.com

To become a supportive patron and receive exclusive content, visit www.patreon.com/ChadLutzke

Other Books by Chad Lutzke

Of Foster Homes and Flies
Stirring the Sheets
Wallflower
Skullface Boy
The Pale White
Slow Burn on Riverside
The Same Deep Water as You
The Neon Owl: Book 1 – When Shit Hits the Van
Cannibal Creator

Collaborations:
Out Behind the Barn (co-written with John Boden)
Wormwood (co-written with Tim Meyer)
The Him Deep Down (co-written with Terry M. West)

Pseudonyms:
Bloodletter: The Hemato Pages Book 1 (written as C.E. Lutzke)

Collections:
Night as a Catalyst
Spicy Constellation & other Recipes
Spinal Remains

Chad has written for Famous Monsters of Filmland, Rue Morgue, Cemetery Dance, and Scream magazine. His short fiction can be found in several dozen magazines and anthologies, and some of his books include: OF FOSTER HOMES & FLIES, STIRRING THE SHEETS, THE PALE WHITE, SKULLFACE BOY, THE SAME DEEP WATER AS YOU, and THE NEON OWL. Lutzke's work has been praised by authors Jack Ketchum, Richard Chizmar, Joe R. Lansdale, Stephen Graham Jones, Tim Waggoner, and his own mother. He can be found lurking the internet at www.chadlutzke.com

I Believe in Gratitude

Thank you to the following people who helped in some way with the creation of this book: Always and forever, my wife Mary. Joe R. Lansdale whose indirect influence is forever in my crime fiction. The author who hired me to do a commission, then changed their mind. Without your indecisiveness, I wouldn't have had the picture prompt which gave birth to this story. Ross Jeffery, Aiden Merchant, and Gabino Iglesias for the blurbs. Hugs to my beta readers: Jennifer Bernardini, Jodi Shatz, Nicole Rubbo, Julie Hiner, Beth Lee, and Aiden Merchant. A *very* sincere thank you to my wonderful patrons: Steve Gracin, Tim Feely, Michael Perez, Dyane Michele, George "Book Monster" Ranson, Liane Abe, Night Worms (Sadie Hartmann and Ashley Saywers), Shannan Ross, Wayne Fenlon, Jamie Goecker, Vitina Molgaard, John J. Questore, Melissa Potter, Jerri Nall, Danielle Milton, Shannon Bradner, Beth Lee, Mary Kiefel, Alyssa Manning, Dirk Gard, Lee-ann Oleski, Mathieu Fortin, Levi Walls, Steve Pattee, Holly Rae Garcia, Phillip Frangules, Sargeras Bolg, Crystal Lake Publishing (Joe Mynhardt), Richard Martin, Crystal Staley, Hunter Shea, Kristyn Kasper, Sheila Porter, Cyndie Randall Lutzke, Jon Cowles, Glenda Magner, Justas Grigas, Missy Kritzer, David Michaele, Alexis Vieira, Tina True Edwards.

Printed in France by Amazon
Brétigny-sur-Orge, FR

15537245R00093